Pleasura
& Realitas

Pleasura & Realitas

The Dialectic of Dominating Impulses

E.L. Stone

Prometheus Books • Buffalo, New York

Published 1993 by Prometheus Books

97 96 95 94 93   5 4 3 2 1

Library of Congress Cataloging-in-Publication Data

Stone, E. L.
    Pleasura and realitas : the dialectic of dominating impulses / by E. L. Stone.
       p.   cm.
    ISBN 0-87975-783-3
    1. Psychhistory. 2. Pleasure principle (Psychology). 3. Reality principle (Psychology). I. Title.
D16.16S75   1993
901'.9—dc20   92-44982
                                                   CIP

Printed in the United States of America on acid-free paper.

Acknowledgments

I wish to thank Victor Blake, Ph.D., of Ottawa and Erik Jackman, Ph.D., of Toronto for their continuing interest and helpful comments. I also express my appreciation to Mrs. Sheila Reynolds for heroic typing efforts on an often indecipherable manuscript. And last, but not least, my thanks to Steven L. Mitchell of Prometheus Books for his patient perseverance and skill in wading through a densely foliated jungle of editing.

Contents

8   Contents

Introduction

"Without history there can be no psychology, and certainly no psychology of the unconscious."

Carl Jung

Human history has proceeded along its course like a great river flowing to the sea from the mountains. Its beginnings are energetic rivulets and trickles, then a coming together into streams and the forming of the river itself. But the flow is not one of consistent speed nor motion: here it is wild and upsurging with rapids, at another it rolls along complacently in calm and ordered tranquillity. Here it clashes with rocks in a torrent of fury and frenzy whipping itself into a white froth; there some obstruction has dammed off a portion, making the waters contained within it pondlike, seemingly serene. But always beneath the placid surface lurks its dynamic potential to be whipped once more into relentless fury, overpowering and consuming all things in its path until again it meets those circumstances that subdue and settle it.

The context of history emerges from human minds and personalities. And just as the river's form and motion are not constant but change as a result of its variable dynamics, so with history whose influencing factors are found in the universal and timeless human impulses.

Sigmund Freud first enunciated these psychic dynamics, and in particular the pleasure and reality principles. Here I have transformed them into the "Pleasura" and "Realitas" impulses. However, lest there be any misunderstanding, this is not a purely Freudian overview of the dynamics of human history. Insofar as history is a reflection of human mind in

9

action, Freud has been the necessary starting point; his general psychoanalytic structurings of mental process are useful guides to understanding.

But it is not an orthodox Freudian viewpoint that is set forth here; rather, it is a far more general approach expanding from Freud to encompass more basic biological considerations, many of which Freud reflected in his categorizing of the mind's components. One essential difference in this work relates to the nature of the *id* and the basic unconscious wish impulses: in this respect the view expressed here is more Jungian than Freudian in that Pleasura is seen as comprised of all the various fabrics of latent and expressed human desire and not simply sexual desire (which is only one element in the catalogue of contents of the Pleasura impulse). Here the Pleasura is seen to comprise the entire spectrum of human impulses, both negative and positive. The Realitas, on the other hand, is seen to be the controlling force, the strong container within which the passions of impulse are stored and kept under sufficient pressure so as not to burst forth. As an example, the Pleasura is seen as manifested in a riotous mob or a revolutionary uprising: the Realitas is seen as reflected in the government and establishment ruling over that mob or group of revolutionaries. This is a very simplistic rendering of the situation.

If the analogy to the Pleasura principle is the *id* in a very general sense, then likewise the Realitas principle can be said to be loosely analogous to the *ego,* and in this work is seen as the ordering principle of human behavior, both the impulse to impose order and the impulse to be ordered. Freud's vision considered the ego as part of the id, that part that deals with the reality of the external world as the means of interpretation and adaptation by the individual. In a similar vein, this work views the Realitas in one sense as a part of the Pleasura. As will be set out in what follows, a major component drive (perhaps the most substantial component) within the overall Pleasura impulse is the basic drive to survival; it hovers over all the rest, waiting finally to descend when self-gratification seems to threaten ultimate destruction of the individual. To that extent, Realitas as the ordering of a human social group into a more or less stabilized entity is viewed as a product of the Pleasura; its means to ensure its own survival.

If we equate the drive for survival with Schopenhauer's "will to live" —the force he saw as the most important underlying principle of existence—our understanding of its significance as a Pleasura factor is further heightened. In speaking of an existing thing, he observed that, "The will to live is the only true expression of its innermost nature."* The drive

---

*Frederick Schopenhauer, *The Will to Live,* edited by Richard Taylor. (New York: Fredrick Ungar Publishing Co.; Doubleday and Co. Inc., 1967), p. 41.

to survival rather than the will to live, this is the essence of organic phenomena (inclusive of humanity). The securing of its interests represents one of Pleasura's primary persuasion tools in the achieving of its ends. In this work we have made an omnibus of all the forces, dark and bright, of the human psyche and id, under the one head, Pleasura, and have done the same to ego under the appellation Realitas.

In considering my arguments some readers may see an oversimplification of the complex issues of the interaction of Pleasura and Realitas: perhaps this is because the interaction of the two impulses is a fairly straightforward process. In certain instances the two forces appear to reflect a Hegelian kind of dialectic, thus reference is made to the "social-psychic dialectic" as a phrase descriptive of this purported interaction. One formulation involves subject groups within given societies rising up to confront and/or overthrow the ruling groups; here the Pleasura-Realitas dialectical confrontation is clear-cut. In the sense that a group in the throes of Pleasura attacks and overcomes an external neighbor, perhaps there is a clearer adversarial dialectical confrontation: this is the kind of confrontation that a Martin Heidegger* would understand and applaud.

Inasmuch as every social group is a macrocosm reflecting the individual human psyche, the question of true adversarial dialectic becomes more blurred when we return to the Freudian guidelines of the ego viewed as part of the id: we thus, in this reference, perceive the eventual emerging Realitas as arising out of the Pleasura and as a more or less advanced part of it. Later, after a crystallization of the two parts, dialectical confrontation between them can arise when the interests of the two become acutely in conflict in a standard Pleasura-Realitas clash, and this despite the fact that the participants are in a sort of parent-child relationship.

The Pleasura-Realitas type of thinking has been presaged by Friedrich Nietzsche in his concept of the Dionysian (corresponding to the Pleasura) character and the Appolonian (corresponding to the Realitas) character. What seems important in such an approach to both history and the phenomenon of human social grouping in Western society in general is that predictability arises as a real possibility insofar as the enigma of human behavior can be said to be predictable. But there is a chance—if merit lies in such an approach—that the onflow of human history could be controllable, to a certain extent.

If there is something new in this work, it is of course not the psy-

---

*Heidegger, a German philosopher and nazi convert, influenced by Edmund Husserl and Søren Kierkegaard, a proponent of the phenomenological method, sought the apprehension of existence through analysis of 'being', and saw existence as a rebellion against nothingness.

chological methodology or the relevant philosophies. Rather it is the thesis that history is the fleshing out of a perpetual skeleton of impulse interaction, namely, that of the principal psychic forces. Further, these two forces themselves individually ascend or decline in the face of certain, governing circumstances. If these premises are valid, then it follows (1) that the past course of human history can be understood thereby, and (2) the paths of future events may be inferred from knowledge of present, influencing circumstances. But this is art, not science. I have over a great many years formulated the views in this work, views that I feel are illustrated by history and are borne out in current events. There is a character in Isaac Asimov's "Foundation" books, one Harry Seldin who, in Merlin-like fashion, prognosticates with detailed precision thousands of years of history of the human race based on a scientific, psychological study of human history. Thankfully that is fiction, for who would want to robotize the human species by having human variability so determined, so "scientific," without choice?

Inasmuch as human beings are by their nature variable, the danger of such ironclad historical determinism outside of fiction is nonexistent. But humankind's future course of history is surely fair game to artful interpretation, based, as it must be, partly on pure guess because of the variability of our natures and personalities, and partly on the perpetual invariability of the impulse content of the human psyche.

1

The Nature of the Dialectic

The Pleasura and the Realitas

The early Christians in the Roman Empire were illustrative of a group in ascendant Pleasura. Their faith, embodied in the new religion they espoused, was so overwhelmingly unifying in the absoluteness of its one and only truth that they resembled a close-knit family within a hostile environment; at the same time they were growing and enlarging their numbers in the rapid spread of their credo. They loved one another like a family; they believed and practiced communal doctrines; they exulted in the true salvation they believed that they and they alone shared. The Christians were an identifiable, adversarial, select group (as they saw themselves) within the surrounding Realitas's manifestation of imperial Rome. As such their potential for rebellion, Pleasura's extreme tool to overthrow a Realitas regime, was in a state of combustibility, so to speak.

In challenging the divinity of the Roman god-kings the Caesars, they were rebelling, albeit not with force, against the most fundamental precepts of the (284 C.E.) Roman Empire within which they were contained. As a result, by the time of the emperors Decius* and Diocletian the establishment's persecution of the Christians as a recognized rebellious minority was well established. Diocletian in particular harshly reinforced the absolutism of the Roman god-king rule and aimed at eradicating this subversive and treasonous element.

But the movement was spreading and with it increases in influence and power. The slaves and oppressed, impoverished masses of Rome were

---

*Killed during a Goth raid into Thrace in 251 C.E.

in a psychological Pleasura state of readiness to accept the Christian doctrine that reinforced their own diminished sense of worth and appealed to their basic survival instincts (though the survival that Christianity offered was in the hereafter). The invitation to belong to a select group that offered them familial love and the status of brothers and sisters was irresistible. Great numbers whom Roman oppression had robbed of the barest self-esteem lay waiting for just such a welcome phenomenon to arrive, like a miracle, and they wholly embraced it, swelling the ranks of the rebellious minority. The body of Christianity was therefore a growing and potent minority group in Pleasura, i.e., in the throes of wanting to arise and assert itself, to overthrow and overwhelm the pagan ruling Realitas regime.

The Roman Emperor Galerius* on his deathbed granted clemency to the Christians. In 311 C.E. Emperor Constantine was won over by realizing that in Christianity lay the unifying force that could cement the Roman Empire and solidify the faltering Realitas regime. A year later, while fighting for Rome against Masentius, he put the Christian monogram on his soldiers' shields, and in 337 C.E. he converted on his deathbed. The metamorphosis was complete within those few years: from rebellious minority in Pleasura, Christianity crossed over to become infused with the ruling Realitas regime.

The notion of certain specific social classes fixed in permanent instinctual time-locks of dialectical confrontation is erroneous: their adverse structuring lasts only for a time, be it short or long, never permanently. There may then be a moratorium of dialectic between them, and they may indeed join forces under the same impulse banner to join issue with some third party who at that moment may embody the contradictory impulse.

Our modern-day case in point regarding the variability of impulse manifestation is the former Soviet Russia. In 1917, incensed "proletarian" working-class masses rose in a successful overthrow of the "capitalist" regime, and with it the capitalist system, in Russia. The prevailing conditions were ripe for such a revolution: the country was bankrupted by an exploitive ruling class, and was further exhausted and starved by a war† in which it could not afford to participate. Dire necessity, extreme privation, and utter resentment were the qualities describing the situation in which the proletariat found itself, and these are precisely the social prevailing conditions that ignite Pleasura's tinder.

---

*He had proposed that those refusing to sacrifice to the Roman god-king should be immediately burnt alive. He died in 311 C.E.

†World War I.

By its "Pleasura" we mean the proletariats will to rise up and engage its rulers; its will to self-preservation and self-aggrandizement; and more, to bloody revenge, to bloody conquest of its "oppressors"; to self-gratification; to all of its romantic passions and desires to break loose from its "repressive" environment and to crush and chew up that environment and to spit out the pieces. In general, the proletariat's Pleasura was its will to self-assertion through violence and cruelty.

As well, Pleasura includes Freud's "Instinct to Master," the will to be the top dog, the will of the Pleasura group to rule and itself to be the Realitas group, i.e., the governing and controlling group (which hitherto had been the "capitalist" ruling class). We will observe hereafter the other rationale of the Pleasura to become the Realitas, that of necessity for self-survival when faced with the prospect of its own self-destruction (i) if allowed to continue on in an untrammelled rampage of ultimate destructive self-gratification, and (ii) if "cut off" practically from negotiations with the external world from which it must derive its survival needs. In such a case it propels out of itself an egolike Realitas to act as a bridge to the external world, and as a controlling and directing governing power over itself.

Thus in 1917 the Russian masses embarked upon their two revolutions to overthrow the ruling Realitas regime. The first revolution did not tap the full power potential of the mass Pleasura unrest: remnants of the former czarist Realitas were even acting as transitional instruments of Realitas transfer of power from authoritarian czarist to republican. The first revolution in fact resulted in a moderate republican government under Kerensky:* but the continuing privations of Russian participation in World War I and the lack of outside help rapidly deteriorated the conditions of the working masses. This time the full extent of the seething mass Pleasura was able to be tapped, this time against the Realitas of the Kerensky government by the resourceful Bolsheviks, and the social revolution of Lenin was successfully effected, the one that lasted over seventy years and ended just recently.

Pleasura is indeed a pent-up force: so long as the lid is kept on, so long as there is more external pressure than internal upward-thrusting pressure, it will remain repressed and under control. It will increase in inverse ratio to the decrease of external pressure. By "external pressure" we mean all of those psychological and physical elements outside the Pleasura, the positive application of which represses it. Such "external pressure" conditions include the application of terror.

The advent of the Bolshevik government in its first few years brought anything but surcease from tribulation and desperate crises for the Rus-

---

*Overthrown November 7, 1917, by Lenin's Bolshevik socialists.

sian masses. The remains of revolutionary Pleasura were ignited when Soviet Russia found itself fighting forces from outside. This phenomenon —preserving Mother Russia—acted as a firebreak to stop the progress of a new upsurge of Pleasura against the new Realitas Bolshevik regime that was unable to relieve the country's economic hardships and distress. Ironically, if the Western world had not sent in expeditionary forces to combat Bolshevism in Russia, it is entirely possible that the Pleasura of discontent of the masses could have, in the natural course of events, boiled over to engulf the Bolshevik rule before the full entrenchment of Stalinist terror smothered it. However, the firebreak of a new national Motherland Pleasura in the masses preempted any feelings of discontent against the regime. The arrival on Russian soil of British, French, Japanese, Polish, and reactionary Russian armies cemented the masses with patriotic enthusiasm and thus bought time, as it were, for the ruling Bolshevik Realitas to institute adequate ironlike repression. In this came the final irony, for the purported Marxist regime of Lenin was ultimately saved by the workers as soldiers: yet Marx had written "The workingmen have no country."* How often into contemporary time has the naive fallacy of this thinking been tragically proven in war and ethnic strife. Workingmen are not Pleasura-free.

Enter Josef Stalin in 1924 after Lenin's death. Like the historically dual alternating psychology of Chinese rulers, Bolsheviks have also had two alternating schools of thought about being open to the West, one for and one against. Lenin had begun to voice the view of the pro school. Stalin was vehemently opposed. He was an ultra apostle of the orthodox communist system, which necessitated being an uncompromising tyrant who used terror mercilessly. Under Felix Dzerzhinsky, the founder of the Soviet Secret Police, mass terror and a governmental fist of steel came down upon the masses not unlike the enormous cruelty with which Stalin destroyed the Kulaks. With the imposition of the first five-year plan in 1928, still more harsh programs were imposed, and the entire country was engulfed in an iron mantle of restriction. There was no counterrevolution: Stalin and his inward-looking regime remained in power despite the many millions of desperate men and women.

The cruel irony was that the government oppressing peasants who grew richer than their neighbors under Lenin's new economic policy (1921) was in theory their own, supposedly a government of the workers, a working-class Realitas as opposed to the former capitalist Realitas overthrown in 1917.

---

*The Communist Manifesto (Part II, "Proletarians and Communists"), Washington Square Press, Pocket Books, 1976, p. 90.

Some seventy years later, the form of this dialectic exhibited in 1917 had changed. This time a strange thing happened: those same masses who had worn the mantle of the working class in 1917 now, by proxy, wore the hat of the capitalist class. The capitalists were gone, but had they been there, the dialectic would have resumed; but this time the Pleasura would not have erupted in the "proletariat"—in theory the present Realitas rulers —but in the "suppressed" capitalists. Since the long-expelled capitalists were absent, the mass yearning after the necessities and luxuries that capitalism had demonstrated it could bring, as opposed to Soviet-style socialism, took the place of the absent capitalist class itself. The dialectic was on again, even though one of the participants was represented by proxy.

Where a dialectical confrontation arises between the two impulses with an apparent vacuum of representation of one of the adversaries, that vacuum will be filled by a proxy "vessel" for the manifestation of the social-psychic impulse in question. Again our example is the current dialectic in the former Soviet Union, which has resulted in an intended neo-capitalistic revolution still progressing at this writing.

Looking back to republican England at Cromwell's death in 1658, another example presents itself. The Realitas government left by Cromwell was republican in theory if not in practice; the private property owners, the draymen, the footmen, the farmers, and all those who had comprised the army of the new model which had trampled the Royalists. Now with Cromwell dead, reaction set in within the masses, resentment at the strict efficiency and puritan rigor, desire for the restoration of seemingly less rigid monarchy. In short, there was a Royalist Pleasura upsurge and the vacuum was filled by the same private property owners, draymen, farmers, and footmen who had cheered Cromwell and the downfall of Charles I. In 1660 the Royalist Pleasura embodied in the republican masses by proxy culminated in the return of Charles II (reigned 1660–1685) and the restoration of a royal Realitas.

However, the dialectic in this peculiarly English type of situation can be seen from a more complex viewpoint as a battle for political Pleasuras. In this it is interesting to digress that the normally naive romanticism of Marx recognized nevertheless that "every class struggle is a political struggle."*

When confronted with Charles I, Cromwell and his followers represented a Pleasura concerned with preservation of property, of what is "one's own," one's property, one's person. If the "ruled" are strong enough, their Pleasura will succeed against a ruling Realitas that seeks to infringe upon "one's own." In effect, Cromwell represented a historical continuation of the Pleasura concern with "property" and inviolability of personal rights.

---

*The Communist Manifesto, p. 73.

To that extent the struggle revolved about the politics of private property ownership.

The documentary foundation for the rights of property and liberty was the Magna Carta. King John (reigned from 1199–1216), a monarch of the type who believed that the country he ruled was somehow his own personal property, was restrained by confrontation with barons whose collective strength exceeded his own. They therefore possessed the cudgel with which to persuade. They were as a class the manifestation of Pleasura in its seeking to protect personal property from alienation and life and limb from violation.

The Magna Carta was the result of this confrontation in which the "ruled" said to the ruler in effect: "Thus far shall you go and no further, without the consent of one's peers." The right of the ruler to dispose of the property and liberty of subjects was thus permanently obstructed by the "ruled." But subsequent Realitas rulers, monarchs, swung back to the position that their Pleasuras overrode all else by virtue of the fact that they were the ruling Realitas. King James I (reigned from 1603 to 1625) went as far as to return to the divinity principle of the Roman emperors, at least so far as royal rule itself was concerned, when he spoke of his "Divine Right" to rule at his exclusive pleasure.

The Commons, the representative assembly of the "ruled" had, by the time of Charles I, come to accept itself as an associate Realitas, privileged by its rights under the Magna Carta to rule and politically protect its private property rights and privileges from kingly incursion. The political confrontation that resulted in a civil war can thus be seen as a confrontation of two Realitas bodies, king and Commons, each with its own Pleasura interest in mind as against the other. The Commons indeed reinforced its position of requiring security from royal incursion in 1628 by the Petition of Right. In effect, Cromwell and the Roundheads were representatives in another sense of the Realitas of the Parliament and its own Pleasura desires. Charles I was representative of the ruling royal Realitas and its position.

On the narrower and more particular political scale, the institution of Parliament apart, the dialectic here was between the Pleasura of the infuriated common masses against the arbitrary Realitas of the monarchy. As we have seen, the Roundheads themselves subsequently became the manifestation of the Realitas, during Cromwell's regime, and the Royalists the possessors of the emerging Pleasura of the suppressed. Within a mere twelve years, with the return of Charles II, the impulse positions were again reversed.

Before going on, we should make reference to an interesting footnote, namely, the Pleasura invocation by Cromwell to rouse the masses to that pitch of spirit required to make of them an army equal to the skilled, chivalrous Royalist opponents. He did so by invoking religion. Here, as with early Christianity in Rome and later with the spread of Mohammedanism, one sees a very effective Pleasura arousal in religion equal in force to the invocation of the "blood." The religion invoked was the common Christianity of both sides, the difference being that Cromwell called upon it as representative of his side. Christianity, utilizing its sacramental "blood" images, is well suited to compete and/or augment traditional "blood" Pleasura invocations.

As we have observed, the incarnation of the impulses is manifest only when the necessary conditions are present. For example, Marx and Engels recognized that the practical application of Marxian principles depended upon "the historical conditions existing at the time."* And in particular, Marx, though vulnerable to naive romanticism, was nevertheless astute in the practical understanding of the "necessary condition"—"potential actualization" relationship. In defending capitalism he noted that "The historical conditions of its existence are by no means given with the mere circulation of money and commodities. It arises only when the owner of the means of production . . . finds the free worker available, on the market as the seller of his labor power. And this one historical pre-condition comprises a world's history."† First, the given group must contain within it a predominance of potential for the one impulse as apart from the other. And the necessary prevailing environmental circumstances must be correct to trigger that potential into actuality. In the case of Cromwell the seething Pleasura of the masses had been roused by Charles I's arbitrary involvement in foreign wars without the consent of Parliament. When Parliament refused him supplies he made illegal demands and sanctions upon individuals, which led to the Petition of Right (1628) further limiting the king's arbitrary rights. The potential for Pleasura within the masses clearly predominated over the impulse to be governed.

Charles seemed to deliberately take every step with a view to further fueling the masses' Pleasura and pour fuel on the flames by any number of "triggering" acts. In 1629 he dismissed the Parliament. He continued illegal monetary levying and sanctions and for eleven years he did not even summon Parliament. He further aggrieved the masses by installing

---

The Communist Manifesto, p. 52.
†*Capital I,* Vintage Books, ed. 1977, p. 274.

William Laud, a supporter of the Divine Right of Kings, as Archbishop of Canterbury.

In 1640, Charles summoned his last Parliament, the Long Parliament. The became the all-important Pleasura trigger mechanism of the masses. Given the opportunity to assemble, it became the hostile, vocal instrument of the masses' Pleasura. Again, Charles, in his almost deliberate refueling of the popular Pleasura, sought "outside" help from Irish Catholics and discontented Scots, which further enraged the masses. Finally, the king went to Nottingham in August 1642, set up the Royal Standard, and the civil war proceeded.

Does all this mean that there is a determinism in the course of human affairs? To a great extent the answer is affirmative. Given a set of circumstances—a given potential plus a given triggering condition or set of conditions—it would seem highly unlikely that the outcome is not thereby a predictable one. However, to the extent that knowledge is a tool —for example, in tampering with, removing, or instilling the necessary external triggering factors—one can say that determinism in individual cases may be modified, removed, or assisted. What cannot be tampered with is "potential": it is either present or it isn't. It is an inherently inviolate part of the nature of the acting agent. This does not mean that the two impulse potentials may not reside side by side within the heart and mind of the individual. It may be that external circumstances dictate which one will quantitatively be in the ascendancy so that a person can be said to be in a state of potential of the one rather than of the other.

At this point it is useful to return for a moment to a discussion of potentiality and its manifestation in actuality. On the most basic level, matter itself from one point of view can be seen as pure "potentiality," its possibilities limitless. However, every potentiality locked into matter may only be unlocked by the presence of certain specific prevailing circumstances necessary to the particular potentiality's actualization, such as specific coldness of temperature to actualize the potential of water to turn to ice. The system and its patterns under which basic matter operates on the infinitely microcosmic level, if you will, are substantially reflected in the macrocosmic world that we recognize. After all, that world is a manifestation of the various potentials of basic matter. Human society is also a manifestation of those potentials and is not exempt in its dynamics from the causal principles of matter as they relate to realization of potential. What these potentials are is not known, and what the essential qualities of matter are is new and always will be a mystery. These problems will forever perplex materialists. It is here posited that all existence is extension of matter, and indeed that the terms "matter" and "existence" are interchangeable. It is here further posited that such phenomena sometimes deemed "dualistic" in nature, such as mind, are not, but rather are examples of the infinitely variable potential structuring of matter with infinitely variable resultant phenomena. These variable phenomena render to humankind their several and varied appearances (resulting from their individual potentialities). It is not intended to digress further into materialistic speculation; however, it is necessary to emphasize our thesis that matter's infinite variety of results is a system common to the microcosmic and macrocosmic scales, and that the understanding of social and psychic phenomena is aided by the understanding of the materialization method: first, there must be potential for a certain something; second, that potential, to be set in motion, requires certain conditions suited or relevant to it; third, the combination of the two results in the manifestation or actualization of that formerly potential certain something.

Thus, if certain prevailing social circumstances are such that a particular potential could be triggered into actualization, if that potential is present then actualization could and indeed should occur. For example, the history of society in Charles Darwin's day was such—in terms of the pressure of the forces of natural science and social thinking attempting to break through the shell of calcified thought—that anyone in possession of the evidence for a theory of evolution would be pressed by his own inclinations and by other people to develop it. Further, such an intellectually stifling atmosphere would goad the more forceful and ingenious thinkers into looking more closely into "other explanations" (if evidence should present itself) than they might otherwise. And so we find the "coincidence" of two men—Darwin and a French scientist—in effect coming forth at the same time with a theory of evolution. Why then? Because the necessary prevailing social circumstances (including scientific enthusiasm for irreverent "discovery") were then just right for men of such similar potential.

Now, returning to the variable manifestations of these impulses, certain considerations must be addressed. The following factors can be summarized as material to the phenomenon of impulse manifestation:

(a) the potentials for specific impulse manifestation vary;

(b) the environments of prevailing social and economic phenomena (which comprise the necessary prevailing circumstances) are temporal;

(c) The term "social group" is used, among other things, to generally cover all ranges of social groupings and classes, from small families through clans, tribes, nations, alliances of nations, and so on.

In order to understand the dynamics of the Pleasura-Realitas dialectic, the human social situation needs to be addressed in terms of how it seems to work.

2

The Human Society

How It Works

Human society is a structure comprised of groups large and small, as well as groups within groups. The dynamic of human society is interaction, first that of the individual and the society, and second of social groups with each other. Human society strives toward the goal of social homeostasis or the feeling of social well-being, real or perceived. All of this overlays the perpetual dialectical struggle of the two impulses, which harbors in the heart of each group. The "overlay" and the impulse-struggle are interwoven and, to a great degree, interdependent.

Real social well-being can be reasonably ascertained on an objective basis by competent, unbiased social scientists applying the generally recognized methods. The "objective" reading of the social sciences is, of necessity, open to error due to the fact that social scientists are human and that they must rely substantially upon interpretation to achieve their results. But obviously such potential error must be considerably less than that of the purely subjective estimate of a group qualitatively assessing its own well-being.

A group's well-being, real or perceived, is dependent upon the satisfaction of two universal Pleasura demands: first, that of *need* and second that of *desire*. Marx, endeavoring to be scientific, assessed the question of need fulfillment of the proletariat by specifying that the workingman's "means of subsistence must therefore be sufficient to maintain him in his normal state as a working individual."* "Necessity" pertains to that which

---

*Capital I, p. 275.

23

is required to substantially support the daily life needs of the individuals comprising the group, such as the need for food, clothing, fuel, shelter, and procreation. "Desire" reflects the plateau of demand above need, i.e., luxury, from minimal comforts or conveniences such as heat marginally in excess of that required to reasonably maintain life, to extravagances such as ornate automobiles and "haute couture." It is "necessity" that is the prime mover of group Pleasura: if homeostatis of "necessity" is perceived by the group to exist, its Pleasura may well become muffled in complacency. If, however, failure to meet the requirement of "necessity" is perceived by the group as a reality or a real threat, group Pleasura will be aroused and thus be susceptible to ignition.

The definitions of necessity and desire must necessarily be blurred due to mass subjective human perception of the two considerations. Blurring is a tried and true strategy of negative Pleasura as it seeks always to confuse legitimate Pleasura "need" requirements, as it were, with negative Pleasura desires. In this regard the blurring tactic is especially effective with regard to luxury objects and their overlap into the area of necessity. Indeed, necessity can be said to be capable of objective determination, whereas desire is in the main a subjective matter and is the constant divining rod of Pleasura. Thus, desire fraudulently appropriates the colors of need to serve the ends of negative Pleasura. This is a universal conundrum perplexing the most lowly individual as well as the most powerful groups or nations: "I 'need' that in the sense that 'I need food and shelter to survive' " becomes "I 'need' in the sense that 'I desire luxury items for my own personal gratification.' "

The other various subject heads of Pleasura-inspired social interaction of human groups (i.e., as apart from purely economic considerations) are also fundamentally predicated upon the universal demands of necessity or desire. Necessity involves *bona fide* requirements, as, for example, for territorial integrity and/or territorial concessions "validly" based upon objective considerations of self-protection and/or economic survival of the group. Desire in the other-than-economic sense involves all other considerations apart from necessity, e.g., power for the sake of power; ancient or new enmity; lust for territory out of consideration for power (apart from any considerations of economic necessity); avarice; passion; malice; cruelty; and generally "will-to-power" objectives, i.e., desire to master for its own sake. "The mind of man is of two kinds, pure and impure: impure when in the bondage of desire, pure when free from desire."*

Internal manifestations of the impulsive-dialectical confrontation (if

---

*From the Maitri Upanishad.

we may so also refer to it) between two groups within one geographical territory or within one society or nation are most often triggered by economic motives, such as job or living-standard dissatisfaction or by direct or indirect oppression. The catalyst is generally an extreme oppression by the Realitas ruling or dominant group (of which we shall speak later) combined with a bankrupt economic system or a perceived or actual unfair economic system, insofar as the Pleasura group is concerned.

One finds that in almost all "triggering" situations a prominent frequent player is economic. It grates against the fundamental heart of Pleasura, which is the impulse to survival. Note that though we talk of two impulses, Pleasura and self-survival, as if they were individual isolated phenomena, this is for convenience only: the impulse to survive is just one part of the Pleasura impulse. Combined with the impulse (or instinct) to survive is its most frequent player in the cast of trigger mechanisms— economic need.

A very narrow but perhaps meaningful approach to the question of frequent cause of Pleasura-ignition could be one mitigating in favor of economic considerations. For example, in Northern Ireland, one might say that the potential for Pleasura-ignition of the indigenous Catholic population is rooted in its question of identity and of being artificially cut off from its blood-brother population to the south. Another igniting factor of the Irish-Catholic Pleasura is its contrary religion to that of the governing Realitas group, which espouses Protestantism: religion, like "blood" and "language" is a substantial Pleasura ingredient.

However, apart from the very real Northern Irish feelings of Catholic alienation in terms of religion and blood, if one confronts the overarching complaints of the Catholic population broadly stated, one can arrive as well at the conclusions that

(1) The Catholic population perceives itself as being discriminated against with regard to jobs, good housing, and other economic needs and privileges. Hand-in-hand with this there appears to be a complaint about a general political inequality that inevitably leads to the self-same economic deprivations or arouses within the Catholic breast a suspicion of such a linkage.

(2) It would be safe to conclude that with the removal of these complaints there would be an appreciable reduction in Catholic Pleasura (though of course this latter phenomenon will not as a result be extinguished). The true causes of Irish-Catholic Pleasura—as it were—will not magically be eradicated with anything less than the ideal of union.

In a Marxist-oriented essay* on Basque dissatisfaction in Spain, the philosopher Jean Paul Sartre speaks of Basque resentment at the Spanish attempts to suffocate its language (language being, like 'blood," a root substance of group Pleasura). He decries the Spanish attempt to de-specialize the Basque (in terms of culture) into a more general, less particular individual culture, more in tune with the centrist philosophy of government which is Spain's own.

But, the reading of the essay indicates that a major underlying fear of the effect of total Spanish domination is an economic one: if all that the centrist Spanish government intends is achieved, the Basques, he demonstrates, will suffer (indeed, they were then suffering) economic deprivation and hardship. Again, the Basque Pleasura in all its natural smouldering resentments could not be suppressed. But the wind blowing upon it from the great bellows of economic dissatisfaction could. The flame could be allowed to smoulder rather than be fanned up into a raging inferno.

In the Second World War, the demonic genius behind the Nazi Gestapo, officer Reinhard Heydrich understood the igniting capability of economic dissatisfaction upon a subdued populace's pent-up Pleasura. In his coldly cynical assessment of the frame of mind of a subject people he concluded that these economic conditions must be addressed significantly. And so, when he was appointed Nazi governor of Czechoslovakia, he proceeded to implement a program of economic improvement of the subjugated Czechs. It worked. His reign became marked with a kind of unrebellious dissatisfaction of the inhabitants.

However, Allied intelligence was also aware of the Pleasura natures, not only of the Czechs, but of the Germans themselves. Fearing the success of Heydrich's program, they had him assassinated in Czechoslovakia one morning on his way to his office. The savage nature of the German negative Pleasura had not been underestimated. German reprisals on innocent Czech civilians were as murderous and brutal as they were speedy: two entire villages—every last man, woman, and child—were slaughtered. This, in turn, in one fell swoop overthrew the complacency of the relative economic well-being enjoyed by the Czech populace. In flowed the outrage and desire to avenge the blood. The latent smouldering Czech Pleasura was thus whipped into a continuing fiery flame of resistance and sabotage. But it had taken that heavy price to counteract the effects of Heydrich's short-term artificially boosted economic upswing.

---

*"The Burgos Trial" in *Life Situations: Essays Written and Spoken*, Random House, 1977.

It thus becomes apparent that at the root of Pleasura itself is, first and foremost, the most basic and elementary of all needs, the need to survive by the obtaining of the necessaries of life, food, and shelter, with all the relevant variations thereof. The necessary commodities are provided by distribution: without a distribution of goods there is little or no chance of survival. Thus the economic factor lies commingled with all the other prime Pleasura considerations, which are on the whole basic, primitive, and elementary, the very foundation stones of Pleasura itself. Pleasura makes economics its blood brother, as it were, for it proclaims, "I must eat to survive, and I *must* survive. . . ."

Probably the most influential Pleasura eruption in the history of the last five hundred years was that of the French Revolution. It was an organized Pleasura on a massive national scale literally overthrowing the Realitas monarchy and spilling over its national borders to spread the message of "Liberty, Fraternity, Equality" throughout Europe. The Pleasura principle enunciated was that the "me" of the common man is as good as the "me" of the privileged man. Perhaps this was wishful thinking, this appeal to mass equality as a natural fact, but it caught on tenaciously with the vast, underprivileged masses, brimming over with, in Nietzsche's word, "ressentiment" (a seemingly justified "ressentiment," in view of the historical facts of deprivation). Their Pleasuras were ready tinder for this sort of spark, and a conflagration was ignited across Europe and indeed the world, and its effect is still being felt.

The foregoing is a general representation of the French Revolution and what it stood for. The French Revolution itself and the successful military upsurge of the country in its aftermath were necessary conditions precedent to the spread of the Pleasura phenomena of revolution and liberal thought and philosophy across Europe, reinforcing the liberal ideals that had been generated within the former American Colonies after the War of Independence.

The important point here is that Pleasura does not erupt without previous igniting causes: though its phenomena and their consequences at first blush often appear to occur in some form of spontaneous combustion, this is not the case. The kindling must be dry, the spark must be set, there must be a draft, only then will the fire ignite. So with the French Revolution and its aftermath.

The necessary prevailing conditions for setting off the Pleasura were (1) economic oppression by the privileged classes upon the masses; (2) a dearth of relief to be obtained from the nobility and clergy who enjoyed tax-exempt privileges resulting in a condition of unfairness and further oppression on the population; (3) unlike the case of the barons and King

John in England, lack of a common cause of interest between the nobility and the Crown with no resultant phenomena of relief for the rights of the masses, such as the Magna Carta; (4) an isolation of the classes from each other to such a degree that the intellectual position of the lower classes was not really known to the nobility and generally was written off by the Realitas as a harbinger of danger; (5) the current and widely espoused liberal and anarchistic ideas in pre-revolutionary France; (6) the extravagances of the self-gratifying Realitas influenced by a wasteful queen Marie Antoinette, and her dutiful minister Calonne who, to please the royal couple, simply rolled debt over into new debt until in 1789 he had to declare the Realitas regime of the monarchy bankrupt; and (7) the country was economically exhausted.

As with Charles I in England, Louis XVI had to call the Estates General together as a tool for the raising of money, and as in England, that portion of the assembly representing the common people proclaimed its sole power. The next historical events are also similar to the English story, with Louis XVI trying unsuccessfully to send home the Estates General. The other steps leading to July 1789 and the attack on the Bastille, the formal beginning of the revolution, won't be detailed here. However, we must touch upon the further prevailing circumstances that pave the way for a Pleasura overthrow of the Realitas, namely, a situation wherein the Realitas force of terror was weakened so that in the balance, there was one iota more of Pleasura's will for overthrow than of Realitas's will and power to enforce its rule.

It is also important to point out the development of indoctrination as a prime cause: the liberalism of the pre-revolutionary thinkers; the brilliant "Encyclopedists" who railed against inequalities of taxation and social justice; the Physiocrats who, in their criticisms of private property, heralded the advent of the collectivist thinking of socialism and even communism; and of course, Jean Jacques Rousseau who implied in his *Social Contract* that breach of the contract was something of a virtue. In fact, socialism's ideas were breeding and multiplying. These ideas and attitudes no doubt played their Pleasura part in inspiring the Oath of the Tennis Court wherein the commoners' representatives vowed to remain until France had a constitution. Their Pleasura urge to take over and rule was taking hold in a most daring way, but daring and audacity are the hallmarks of Pleasura on the rise.

When Marshal de Broglie, the queen's choice to counter the revolt in Paris, would not fire upon the French masses, the will of the Realitas to impose and perpetuate itself by force was clearly broken. Paris in revolt was the equivalent of the Tiananmen Square uprising of 1989 in China, the only difference being that the will of the Chinese Realitas to maintain order by force exceeded (by far) the energy of the Pleasura revolt. This was also the equivalent to the old Realitas's attempted coup in Moscow in 1990: here again the soldiers would not fire on the people, and no leader of the coup had the will to do so. This was countered by the demonstrated will of the Chinese Realitas to maintain order by ruthless imposition of force.

As for the subsequent spread of Pleasura's more positive aspects of humanitarianism and liberalism—these ideas had already long been fomenting in Europe since the days of the great peasant revolts: and though they had been latent all those years they were the underlying dry tinder that was necessary for flames to ignite. The spark itself was the French Revolution and its strength of will and purpose: to ignite all of Europe in a Pleasura-reveling conflagration of liberalism. The watchword to come out of all of this was the principle that all men are created equal and have equal rights. The cynic would include as well the long-smouldering desire of the oppressed masses, since the days of the peasant revolts, to get revenge (a potent Pleasura theme) against their long-time oppressors, to even the score on a wide scale. This is the nature of the dialectic understood by Marxists in their interpretation of historical dialectic situations as being always, "in a word, oppressor and oppressed . . . in constant opposition to one another." Carrying on "an uninterrupted now hidden, now open fight. . . ."* Marx therefore sees the dialectic between "freeman and slave, patrician and plebian, lord and serf, guild master and journeyman"† as perpetually that of oppressor and oppressed, as if there could be no other designations.

Today, it is taken as an undeniable given that by virtue of being human each of us inherits a legacy of equality with all other humans (whether they are of equal ability, intelligence, talent, etc., or not). That is, the message of equality has been subverted from the case of the gross inequity of arbitrary, artificial class barriers to a blanket universal Pleasura fiat that all humans are mysteriously equal and should be so regarded. This message appeals to the Pleasura in the masses of humankind who by nature are not fitted with the gifts and abilities of others: they thus seek "damages" as it were, for the misfortune of the omission of talents not given to them by nature. They require that they be treated as if they hadn't been so deprived. This "damages" approach comes likewise from the same Pleasura message that talks of all humans having certain given natural "rights," whereas in reality, all humans have certain

---

*The Communist Manifesto, p. 58.
†Ibid.

natural expectations, some of which may be reasonable, others not. These expectations have, in the last two centuries, come to be evidenced as legal rights in many Western constitutions as a last permanent lingering influence from the French Revolution. Even at the height of the British Empire the voice of its junior minister in Gladstone's third government (Joseph "Joe" Chamberlain) could be stridently heard in echo of the French revolutionary eruption of liberal ideals, "The divine right of peers is a ridiculous figment. We will never be the only race in the civilized world subservient to the insolent pretensions of an hereditary caste."*

All this from one great eighteenth-century volcanic eruption of Pleasura. And yet, the prime cause of the French Revolution was the bankruptcy of France, the economic disaster to which mismanagement and parasitism by the ruling Realitas regime had led it. As fundamental to the revolution as the Pleasura principles that were ignited was the necessary prevailing circumstance of unmitigated economic disaster on a national scale. Indeed it may be said: "He who feeds me leads me." Likewise, "He who does not feed me will not long lead me."

Notwithstanding the apparent "spontaneity" of a group's negative Pleasura outrage resulting in aggression upon a neighbor, at the base of the great pile of its smouldering motivation is usually one that is by its nature an igniting substance, namely, lust for a beneficial economic asset obtainable by conquest. True power rests on an economic base. No conqueror boasts of reigning over sheer desert devoid of any populace, animals, vegetation, or mineral wealth. There must be economic productivity upon which the conqueror can draw or can hope to draw. However, it sometimes happens that the conqueror has been mistaken and that conversely he is required to support the conquered territory. But this is sheer accident, for conquest and the establishing of power imply power over something of value economically or statistically, otherwise the subject territory is not "worthy" of the conqueror's expenditures and efforts of his domination. The one exception is when the conqueror has deemed the necessity (and not luxury) of this economically unproductive conquest is justified for protection purposes, e.g., a barrier against attack.

This is not to say that a nation in a state of Pleasura setting out to conquer another for the motive of revenge, let us say, consciously ranks economic benefit as its equal motivation. But it is there, and implicit in the conqueror's understanding is due economic consideration to be received for his efforts. All great empires such as Rome and Macedonia were great for other fundamental reasons because of and so long as eco-

---

*Robert K. Massie, *Dreadnought*, New York: Random House Inc., 1991, p. 232.

nomic benefit—in the form of direct and indirect tribute—flowed to the conqueror so that its net worth was truly improved by the conquest with the addition of a true economic asset (though of course, it wasn't necessarily blatantly looked at or proclaimed in that fashion).

A pertinent example that comes to mind is the Rome of the time just after the fall of Carthage. This is the period to which we may have recourse to refer to later, the Rome that became intoxicated with the Pleasura excesses of money and all the myriad opportunities that were arising to acquire it. One of the most effective means was conquest resulting in the eastward expansion of the empire in the post-Carthage period with Rome extending its rule by warring. In so doing, it utilized its dominion over its vanquished as an expedient means of siphoning off plunder, the capital and treasure reserves of the conquered, making the individual conqueror-generals rich and increasing the affluence of Rome itself. Later, with the end of the economic benefit-flow to the ruling country, there came a dislodging of the keystone of that supporting arch of factors holding the empire aloft, with a resultant weakening of the entire superstructure.

And looking at humanity's long history of kings and lords and their Pleasura-inspired dominations and conquest, in effect these royal and noble personages were, in their own way, in the real-estate business. Belligerency and invasions led to the acquisition of more real estate by the war lord. This real estate brought along its own income-producing tenants, namely, taxpaying subjects. A reading of history shows that the conquerors, like any real-estate entrepreneur, were also usually in need of cash for further acquisitions: in their case, however, the equivalent cost of acquisition was the cost of the army that would be acquiring the new real estate by force.

The British imperialists of the latter part of the nineteenth century were nothing if not pragmatic realists, and when the occasion arose they were prepared to take action. At the height of the British Empire, Joseph Chamberlain, ever the stereotypical no-nonsense English businessman, referred to the empire as a vast real-estate holding. As colonial secretary he declared that it is not enough to occupy great tracts of the earth's surface; like a diligent landlord, the holder must develop the real estate.

The interaction of groups is, among other things, based upon what could be called the universal group search for social homeostasis, be it either real or perceived. As we have noted, real homeostasis begins and ends "objectively" with the reasonable satisfaction of necessity, i.e., substantial support of life needs. Perceived or qualitative social homeostasis begins but does not end at the plateau immediately surpassing satisfaction of basic life needs, i.e., the plateau of comfort or "reasonable" expectation as an accompaniment to the satisfaction of necessity. The ancient Gordian-

Knot problem raises its head concerning the subjective interpretation of "reasonable," which is most often the method of choice in interpreting what that term means.

Apart from autocracies, a human group is predominantly a reflection of the most universal individuals comprising it: to that extent, the phenomenon of the social-psychic state of the group is, though unintentionally, democratic. The group takes its psychological coloring, its philosophical bent, and all other relevant attributes from these most universal individuals, or, the most representative individual of the group. If these individuals are under the sway of a particular leader or ideology, it follows that so goes the group.

As individuals vary in nature, so do groups. And what is sauce for one group is not necessarily sauce for another. What comprises potential for Pleasura in one group is not necessarily the potential for the same in another. For example, the type of abusive working conditions that many lower-echelon workers in India submit to daily would never be tolerated by American workers whose boiling point is much lower than that of their Indian counterparts when it comes to such conditions. The same is true regarding the necessary prevailing circumstances required to manifest these potentials. Thus, though the two principles of Pleasura and Realitas are universal, their being called into existence is based largely upon relative and variable factors.

The spectrum of Desire (rationalized as "necessity") is inclusive of desire for power attainment of the "blood" group over others who, not being of the "blood," are thought to be inferior and therefore fair game for all the intents manifest in the Pleasura. At the extreme end of this "not-of-the-blood" spectrum (which is really a range of potential victims) the individuals are perceived to be nonhuman "things" thereby freeing the Pleasura from its last and strongest shackle, conscience.

In primitive and aboriginal tribes it is common to find their language describing themselves as "the people" and all others outside the tribe, by implication, as not "people" but something less: things, animals perhaps, objects for conquest, and so on. To the ancient Japanese (and to a certain extent with lingering traces evident even today) outsiders were all "barbarians," equivalent almost of the Abominable Snowman. In Nazi Germany, non-Germans or "Auslanders" were categorized in degrees of non-humanness. This latter perception undoubtedly greatly aided the morale of the S.S. exterminators of the inmates of Auschwitz and its sister camps by dulling their consciences.

Quite often the blood-proclaiming group paradoxically manifests symptoms of uncertainty as to the quality it loudly proclaims. These are things that can be observed indirectly. For example, when European Caucasians made cultural contact with the aborigines of the New World, they categorized European-aboriginal blood-mixing in terms of animal breeding: one would assume that the subjective category of animal to be mixed would be reflective of the categorizer. The Europeans, in particular the British, used the noble animal figure of the horse as their analogy, thus, mixed racial types came to be known as "mixed" or half-breeds. In Nazi Germany, such blood-mixing was given a much lower term of reference: it referred to racial mixing as "mongrelization," and mixed racial types as "mongrels." It would make an interesting study to pursue the psychological aspects underlying the Pleasura need to "blood-boast" as it were. Does this Pleasura phenomenon overlay a still deeper Pleasura issue, namely, fear related to a racial insecurity in terms of one's racial worth?

In the phenomenon of conquest the chief necessary condition for a Realitas manifestation is quite obviously submission, voluntary or involuntary, of the subject group to the conqueror's will. The submission can be achieved politically as well as militarily, e.g., annexation voted into effect by plebiscite of the annexed, as with the Anschluss of Austria by the Nazis in 1938. This was a combination of voluntary and involuntary submission in that many of the German subjects of Austria seemed to have voluntarily leaned toward annexation with the German Fatherland. Hitler, in his incarnation as the representative voice of the Germans under Austrian imperial rule, railed against the Czech element that was so distasteful to Germans, as was the cosmopolitanism of Vienna; in general in Marxian fashion he tried to present to the world an impression of the Austrian Germans as a subjugated people. This Germanic voluntary submission phenomenon was offset against the involuntary submission of the many unwilling elements in Austria to Anschluss, including many Austrian non-Nazi Germans.

An example of a more predominantly voluntary (though passive) submission to be ruled can be found in Rome following the assassination of Julius Caesar. A condition necessary to manifest the impulse to be ruled is the pretext of faith and confidence in the potential leader. This feeling was engendered in the wild promulgation of the exploits of hero generals, such as Caesar, thereby stimulating a certain hero-worship of the "strong" man, a cult of personality. Further, the populace was beginning to be "spoiled" by strongmen or pseudostrongmen seeking its support and appealing to its Pleasura: for example, Caesar himself held extravagantly public festivals to cater to the desires of the masses to be fed and entertained.

The desire to be ruled is also nourished by political and social instability. When Caesar was made dictator for ten years in 46 B.C.E., his powers were literally those of a monarch, and "republican" Rome was bowing its head to an autocratic yoke. When Caesar was assassinated, the ruling body, the senate, was demoralized. Assassinations, intrigues, plots, all of these elements of instability undoubtedly made themselves so felt in the psyche of the Roman masses that by the time Octavian arrived, demolished his opponents, and took command in "strongman" fashion, the mood of the populace was receptive to if not desirous of being ruled by a strong Realitas, a monarchy. This is not to say that the impulse "to be ruled" means of necessity to be ruled autocratically. No. Rather, it is the impulse of the id, if you will, to have order between it and the external world. It is the universal impulse to be ruled. In the case of Rome, by the time Octavian took control, the populace was ready to submit to his "strongman" rule and its authoritarian implications: the spirit of the republic was decidedly in eclipse. At the base of it all was a Pleasura desire of the masses to survive the whole unstable mess: their Pleasura, long dominated and repressed by strong Realitases, sought salvation in an even stronger and hopefully more beneficent Realitas.

3

Pleasura:

A Review

Let us pause at this point to review our understandings of the impulses. The definition of Pleasura, briefly stated, is the fundamental tripartite impulse to

(a) self-survival,

(b) self-improvement,

(c) and self-gratification.

Parts (a) and (b) can be tested objectively as well as subjectively; (c) can only be tested subjectively.

Another approach—a narrower approach—at a definition would be to describe Pleasura as the impulse to ingest one's external environment. It is possibly the oldest organic impulse, and is exhibited by the one-celled ameba, with its fingerlike pseudopodia, that blindly gropes about until a manageable piece of its environment falls into its grasp whereupon the matter is immediately ingested into the organism. This is the blind, inflexible driving survival impulse of the organism which takes priority over all and any other impulses. This is the impulse chained to every organism, from the lowest to the highest.

In man, these are the driving forces of the id, and more: they are the determined compulsions to survive by controlling the environment as well as absorbing it. But still more, there is the *einsatz-gruppen* part of the impulse of Pleasura, as it were, an irrational compulsion to waste that portion of the environment not absorbed or desired to be absorbed; such waste is usually manifested in violence and savagery. This wasteful compulsion is reflected in part in Freud's categorization of the instincts as aggression, cruelty, destruction, and so on. But it is more: in its extremes, it is in fact the rapacious blind desire to engorge the external environment, and by so doing one supposes that by extension the final aim is to become the environment itself. However, it is also the force that compels an individual on not only to self-gratification, but to self-realization. The latter case demonstrates the paradox of Pleasura: it is both the most constructive and the most destructive impulse.

Throughout, where we use qualitative epithets such as "constructive," "destructive," "negative," or "positive" in their value sense, these are being applied relatively, that is, in the human-chauvinistic perspective. In particular, we will refer to the reference to the "good" in Pleasura as that which aids and augments the self-realization aspects within human nature as apposed to brutish self-gratification and the Nietzschean qualities. In this sense there is almost an equivalence between gratification motivation and negative Pleasura; but in a sense this is overly simplistic in that every aspect of the spectrum of values is itself a spectrum from negative to positive, like the spectrum of Pleasura itself.

We have also noted that Pleasura is the impulse that leads to revolt and revolution; self-determination; self-aggrandizement; and from there externally to domination and/or savagery of the external environment; crimes, (e.g., murder, rape, and so on); and at the same time, democracy. So far as humanity is concerned, Pleasura is the romantic impulse at its most constructive, and the maniacal at its most destructive.

In relation to the impulses, we have addressed the considerations of potentiality and actuality. The potential for controlling domination to manifest itself in an individual or group thought and emotion requires prevailing conditions, without which it remains latent. Necessary prevailing circumstances directly address the individual Pleasura: such as basic needs and wants, pride in blood and territory, fear of diminished safety or pride, perceptions of individual or group insult, perceptions of individual or group superiority, will to power, and so on.

Proportionally, the greater the domination of negative Pleasura on an individual or group psyche, the less reason is left within that psyche. Pleasura (in its negative phase) and reason are two unhappy bedfellows: the one will always seek to dominate or evict the other.

To the proponents of Pleasura—and though they may not call it by that name there are many—reason is anathema. Reason mitigates against the granting of freedom to the Pleasura, the handing over to it of unbridled reign. Reason runs contrary at every bit of license thrown to the hungry enslaver and therefore emerges as the object of scorn and distrust by negative Pleasura. The proponents of Pleasura see reason as disenchantment and disillusion: they alone see reason as the enslaver. Hermann Goering expressed this sentiment best when he declared, "Whenever I hear the word intellectual, I go for my gun."* (This last remark is not to imply any necessary correlation between intellectuals and reason, though undoubtedly, in Goering's mind, the two may have been connected.)

Realitas, on the other hand, is the two-part impulse of order: the active impulse to command and to order, and the passive impulse to obey and to be ordered. Realitas comes both before and after eruption of Pleasura with its consequential disruption of the environment and the resultant need for new environmental restructuring. The group in a state of Realitas is the ordered group. At the top is the instrument of the Realitas, the commanding individual or group, while within are the equally if not more important instruments: the commanded and the obeying. Realitas is most commonly experienced by citizens in relationship with government. "Organized government is an almost universal phenomenon."†

A group or society in a state of Realitas has a vested interest in its self-perpetuation. Order, of whatever kind, seeks to perpetuate itself in a linear fashion. In this regard, it is inimicable to the expression of Pleasura through the individuals comprising the commanded group or the group itself as a whole, for the two are paradoxical adversaries, and at the best live together in wedded un-bliss. The paradox of the Realitas is this, like the ego, it is a product of the id-like Pleasura.

We have come to understand that a group is either substantially in a state of Pleasura, or substantially in a state of Realitas. Although a group is in a substantial state of one or the other, that state is not there to the exclusion of the other. There is no 100 percent saturation of a group: it is, however, a majority and predominant saturation, overpowering the other, and giving the group its current impulse character.

What it comes down to is that, paradoxically, Pleasura is the most important factor in the development of humankind's society in an onward and upward path toward human self-realization, while at the same time being the most significant element in the destruction of that same society. This results from its unbridled negative will to savage the external environment, primarily the external group(s) that, for whatever reasons, it has pinpointed as a target in its desires to absorb, control, savage, and/or destroy.

The social-psychological dialectic results from the fact that the two

---

*Kurt Ludke, *I Knew Hitler,* ca. 1939.

†Bernard Crick, *In Defense of Politics,* New York: Penguin Books, 1973, p. 186.

impulses are constantly interacting, each seeking dominance over the other in order to achieve its respective purpose. (Again, this is always subject to the paradox that, at a certain point, if and when Pleasura recognizes that its most basic survival is at stake if its will is allowed to continue a chaotic and unbridled reign, it will survive by giving rise to an ego-like Realitas, drawn from its own elements.)

4

The Dialectic as a Phenomenon of Claustrophobia

The Contained Versus the Container Environment

In a sense the situation of the interaction of the two forces can be reduced to a discussion of claustrophobia of sorts. That is, there is that which contains, and there is that which is contained. That which contains, namely, the Realitas, does so as a container, as a control upon the freedom of the contained Pleasura reducing it from its desired absolute, unhindered freedom to controlled restriction. The latter is in a passive state of Realitas, i.e., that of "being commanded." Marx recognized this pent-up energy within the class he so despised—the bourgeoisie. Yet he had to admire its uprising against eons of economic and social oppression. For Marx, "the bourgeoisie was the collective hero of a romantic tragedy. Like many heroes of romantic tragedies, the bourgeoisie rose from low estate against enormous odds, burst its chains and hurled the older masters from their seats of power. Like many heroes of romantic tragedies—Prometheus and Faust—the bourgeoisie was possessed of an enormous and restless energy."* In the main, Marx acknowledges that this energy was positively spent. "It has accompanied wonders far surpassing Egyptian pyramids. . . . It has conducted expeditions that have put in the shade all former migrations of nations and crusades. . . . It batters down all Chinese walls."† Marx did not see fit to praise the fact that unlike his chosen hero, the proletariat,

---

*The Communist Manifesto, p. 28.
†Ibid.

the bourgeoisie did not have to overthrow its chains by the negative phenomenon of bloody revolution, but by skill, daring, enterprise, and many of the virtues hailed by Calvinists—undoubtedly a less romantic (and bloody) way to get to the top.

Paradox again raises its head here in that if the individual Pleasura group feels negative to its Pleasura container, how are Pleasura phenomena such as repelling of invaders seen as consistent with the claustrophobic antagonism? One would think that the "restrained" Pleasura would welcome the invader or be indifferent to it, as in the case of the Roman populace confronting the barbarian invasions of the third and fourth centuries.

The force of individual Pleasura submits if the Motherland or Fatherland as an overriding Pleasura consideration prevails. As in the case of Soviet Russia in World War II, the oppressed people rise to the defense of the country as if there had been no oppression upon them. H. G. Wells, in his *Outline of History,* talks of the tribal instinct of humankind, which leads him to attach himself to something larger: cities, states, and the like. Wells saw human beings as inclined to subdue their own criticisms in the face of attacks and criticisms of others against larger entities that enclose their lives. Wells postulates that humans have a fear of isolation that could result in the distraction of the system that contains them. Here we would see such a fear of isolation as being another hat worn by the impulse to be ruled. It is almost the contrary of the claustrophobic sentiment, and if stimulated, it works to save the "container" rather than dislodge or destroy it. But there must be something more. For the claustrophobic element to firmly anchor itself, there must be an extended period of disenchantment with and loss of hope in the Realitas rule, as in the case of Rome in the later barbarian invasions. There is also an added contemporary factor in the equation, which was lacking in ancient history —modern mass communications. Stalin and Hitler had radio and the press to disseminate mass Pleasura inculcation. Ancient Rome, however, had no such media capabilities: word of mouth carried infrequent and petty news, long after the event, to farflung and dissatisfied peasants.

But a further thought emerges: no sooner does one impulse object established itself than another is sought in its wake. No sooner does the ruler's desire for imposition of rule upon it occur than dissatisfaction arises. That is, upon imposition of a sought-for Realitas, the Pleasura becomes claustrophobic, as it were, and the road to seeking its overthrow is begun. There seems to be a constant state of instability when it comes to satisfying instincts.

As opposed to the Realitas born of the Pleasura, there is the externally imposed Realitas as, for example, by conquest. In such a case, the subdued group with the externally imposed conqueror's Realitas becomes the Pleasura group in a classic state of dialectic and adversarial interaction with the Realitas. The former Realitas of the subdued group, the former ruling element, becomes absorbed into the overall Pleasura group though infrastructure custom may pertain within the new Pleasura group wherein the old Realitas is still somehow recognized by the balance of the group as having special shadowy Realitas status. An obvious example is the case of prisoners of war: though their conquerors are the de facto new governing authority, nevertheless the old hierarchy of command is still maintained among the prisoners.

The question then arises as to the bipartite nature of the dialectic: in particular, in the case of a Realitas emerging from a Pleasura, can there be a true dialectic in that the two are parent and offspring as it were? In the case of a Pleasura movement in revolution against the Realitas, if it succeeds, its leadership elements generally form the whole of the nucleus of the new Realitas. In this, it is also by nature a Realitas that emerges from the Pleasura, ego-like, to control the internal and communicate with the external. It is a practical imposssibility for an entire group to govern and control except through leaders and governors who become the new Realitas. Can a dialectical confrontation arise here also? The answer to both questions is yes. The relationship of parent and offspring does not necessarily supersede the vital energy thrusts of the two impulses so as to submerge all confrontation. The only difference here to a traditional parent-offspring relationship is that normally the parent is the manifestation of the Realitas, imposing discipline upon the child, and the child, in turn, is the repository of the Pleasura. Here, however, the parent is the Pleasura group and the offspring, as it were, is the Realitas, a necessary Realitas so far as the Pleasura group is concerned. Just as the classical parent-offspring relationship does not preclude dialectic impulse interaction, so in the case of turnabout parent-offspring relationship—if we may so call it—where the order of the impulses is reversed, the impulses themselves still maintain primacy over the parent offspring status and are unaffected by any questions of turnabout. Pleasura, though it heralds family as an instinctual interest consideration, is no respecter of it in questions of ultimate self-interest. When the self-interest of the American colonists got in the way of their relationship with the mother country, England, self-interest won. And one need only think of the many illustrations of the bitter squabbling and hatred of children fighting over the spoils of deceased parents' estates to see how effectively self-interest rises to rope off family interest.

So that in the case of Pleasura-born Realitas, which we shall here for illustrative purposes take the liberty of calling Realitas P.B. (Pleasura Born), the social-psychological dialectic is very much alive and thriving as in the case of imposed Realitas. We shall later refer again to the apparent contradiction regarding parent-offspring type of adversity when we view it in relation to the question of the cyclic pattern of the impulses.

Examples of Realitas P.B. can be found in the democratic (and even nondemocratic) systems whose Realitases have emerged from revolutionary Pleasura groups that have succeeded in overthrowing an imposed Realitas, e.g., a colonial one. Even though the resultant Realitas has emerged from, indeed been born of, the revolutionary colonized group-in-Pleasura, nevertheless the old dialectical confrontation remains. In resultant autocracies, of which the history of Central and South America are rampant, violent overthrows of the Realitas regimes seem a commonplace phenomenon. In the democracies of North America, however, the dialectic is nonviolent but there nevertheless. In America the dialectic's dangerous edge between ruling Realitas and the governed masses is blunted by the tools of controlled grumbling and humor so that it is commonplace to always make impinging references to the politicians who govern and to the democratically elected government itself, and to maintain these as subject matter of jests and lampoons. These are the recognized and accepted democratic values that permit the outflow of dangerous excess steam, a positive Pleasura form of control upon the negative, aggressive urge against the Realitas government.

The case of an externally imposed Realitas system is more straightforward in terms of the observable dialectic and does not require many examples. The paradox in externally imposed cases is that when the Realitas is overthrown, it is replaced by the Realitas P.B. and the old dialectic is resumed between ruler and ruled and perpetuated in new forms, subject to all the old rules.

It should be understood that the social-psychological dialectic has variations on the historical themes. For example, in seventeenth- and eighteenth-century Europe the National Powers were engaged in imposition of rule over the workers. Russia, for example, externally imposed its Realitas upon a group of subject constituents—e.g., Ukrainians, Tartars, Cossacks, Estonians, etc.—and the same can also be cited for England, Sweden, France, Austria, and so on, during this period of history. This "internal" pattern of the major European nations led to the National Power idea that has prevailed even into contemporary history. These "power systems" in turn become imposed Realitases upon the weaker and lesser "powers" who, in turn, out of Pleasura fear for survival, are seen in the history of the nineteenth and twentieth centuries to submit themselves regularly to Realitas ordering by the respective "national powers," such externally imposed Realitases being implemented by the euphemistic "alliances": treaties of "mutual cooperation," "requests" for external intervention, and so on. The National Power phenomenon was effected by transferring the power that formerly reposed in monarchs to the countries themselves, so that one spoke about the "power of France" as opposed to the power of Louis the XVI, for example. The individual weaknesses, inabilities, and self-indulgent Pleasuras of monarchs of the seventeenth and eighteenth centuries left the effective Realitas's ruling powers in the hands of ministers and bureaucrats who continued to maintain government and inter-government relationships while the respective monarch strutted his on national stage for the time allotted him. The Pleasuras of nations and the resultant "national interest" began to eclipse the glory of individual monarchs. Ministries and secretariats became the perpetual continuing repositories of policy and Realitas powers, becoming mini-Realitases of their own, presumably with their own Pleasura power interests and ambitions, even into the twentieth century. There is more truth to the Machiavellian bureaucratic manipulating of ruling politicians as satirized on the BBC-TV series "Yes, Prime Minister," than meets the eye.

In the modern world of the near future, the reality of meaningful international power will likely be economic power. By analogy to military power, the nation that possesses the strongest and most formidable economy will be the one most able to impose its will upon the rest. An economic hierarchy of lesser and less fortunate entities shall, in feudal-like fashion, spiral around and up to the stronger economic "protector" nations who shall dominate. Both the Pleasura survival needs and Realitas desire to be ruled shall express themselves in economic unions and blocs dictated by the strongest member(s). But economic considerations are not philanthropic: Pleasura dictates that only those who are useful shall be given access to the economic "goodies." In all likelihood, those who are useful are already economically strong and/or of strategic value. Like their medieval counterparts, the participants in the new economic feudalism will share in the special dispensations and privileges granted by the new feudal lords within their common-market fiefdoms (euphemistically referred to by such terms as "regional trading blocs"). The new dominant Realitases will be the exclusive economic unions. However, the Pleasuras of ethnic interest will maintain as forces to be reckoned with and as the weak links in the new chains of economic unity being forged. As a case in point, one need only take note of the contemporary French and British fears of a strong Germany dominating such a union.

Throughout the balance of this work, no effort will be taken to stop at each individual case of Realitas to categorize it as P.B. or "classical." Rather, the informal tone of general reference to the dialectical phenomena shall be carried on. But this must not be misconstrued as overriding the necessary initial understanding of the various dialectical component parts and their natures or the nature of their origins.

The state ultimately sought and desired by human Pleasura is one of absolute, unrestricted freedom of movement and action. It is the undisciplined, free-ranging state of the ameba: unenclosed, unrestricted, seeking to ingest whatever it can and to that extent master of its environment. Freedom brings with it a certain control of one's environment, and to that extent freedom brings a sense of power if not power itself. And power is music to the ears of Pleasura, for Pleasura desires to master, to control, and in the end to control completely. To that extent Pleasura itself contains within it the living seeds of Realitas.

Earlier we suggested a further look at the apparent contradiction of parent-offspring adversity. One might ask here how that proposition tallies with the claustrophobic image of a Pleasura trying to break out of and eliminate the confining Realitas. That is, in Realitas P.B. the Pleasura itself, out of its own perception of necessity for survival purposes, gave rise to the Realitas. It seems a contradiction for Pleasura to be opposed to and try to destroy its own creature does it not?

The answer is that once the component parts of the dialectic are there, it begins again notwithstanding the nature of the origin of those parts. Pleasura is an impulsive, not a reasoning creature. The danger of anthropomorphism is that in treating intangibles as we would acting and reacting people, we often go one step further in seeking to actually imbue the intangible with the components of the human who is being referred to only by analogy. The Pleasura does not sit down and start to reason about the logic or illogic of attacking its own creature. Rather, given the circumstances of an enclosing Realitas, it reacts: it is an impulse, a psychological force acting in a determined fashion in response to given circumstances. Attacking of its own Realitas P.B. is not a contradiction to its nature or its dynamic.

The pattern can be seen as a cycle, i.e., the Pleasura gives rise to Realitas, which it overthrows and gives rise again to Realitas, and so on. In an objective sense, the Pleasura's actions are frequently absurd: but absurdity is one part of its nature.

The more that reason (the Golem of Realitas) is subdued, the greater is the power of Pleasura and the wilder its whirling dervish dance of freedom, as Jekyll-and Hyde-like, it metamorphoses from positive to negative. Pleasura also understands "freedom" to mean total license. When license runs against reason, its course is one of insanity, and though it be license it isn't freedom. The more that liquor overpowers the drunkard, the more his sense of imagined "freedom." His lack of inhibiting restraints develops and Pleasura is allowed freer and freer reign until insane, drunken, random acts of gratification and nonsense result. The more that the mentally ill person's reason is clouded, the greater the "freedom" of Pleasura manifested in acts of insanity.

Two points should be made here. When we talk here of "negative" or "constructive" qualifications to the impulses, we are speaking relatively. Of course, our values viewed in this regard are controlled by our humanity-chauvinism, as it were. Relative to other species, to the rest of the planet, or to the solar system the fate of humanity might be a matter of complete indifference or even, in the light of our destructiveness, it might well be an outcome earnestly to be desired.

Second, the "claustrophobia" idea can be taken to cover a larger canvass, namely, humankind's general feeling of constraint and containment due to its reliance upon and restriction to the environment as a source of food and other necessities. This "claustrophobic" sense may well be as innate and primary a basic Pleasura property as survival. Next to survival (and indeed sometimes overstepping it) comes humankind's primal Pleasura outcry for "freedom" and its perennial and everlasting search for it, a search that will never end. Nor will humanity in the most basic sense ever indeed be "free" for it will always be "chained" to the society within which it lives, and its people are physically chained to their bodies and reliance upon the external environment, both natural and artificial, and its whims. Freud sees the supreme power of nature and the limitations of the human body as being ultimate sources of human suffering that we, albeit reluctantly, accept.

There is an interesting portrait by Franz Hals in which the subject, though posed with face toward the viewer, has his eyes fixed in an annoyed manner toward the edge of the picture. The annoyance of the subject seems directed at his confinement by the very picture frame itself. There is a recognizable pent-up Pleasura energy that the viewer can instinctively understand, and a certain catharsis is thereby experienced. Hals's subtle rendering of the message of the restrained individual antagonistically contemplating the source of his discomfort, namely, the narrow confines of the restraining environment (the very picture frame itself), is perceptive. So much is rendered in that indignant glance that, although the portrait is not of a man in motion, nevertheless it can be considered to have vitality, which arises from the interaction between the confined and the confining environment.

That is not to say that all art is merely a therapeutic vehicle for the outlet of the pent-up energies of the confined: that is not the total answer. But we are not concerned with the broader question of esthetics.

Among other things, the purpose of art is to help us to understand the nature of things as artists have the talent and capability of seeing them for us. This in itself is a Pleasura end inasmuch as it helps us to absorb (through perception and understanding) whole essences of beings and things of our environment. Nietzsche speaks of the "will to power as being like a stomach in its absorptive nature," and to a great extent, this simile is apt in the understanding of the nature of the Pleasura, even in its positive aspect.

It might be said that one of the ends of art is to act as a form of escape from confinement; a broadening or a greater encompassing of the external environment by intellectual absorption. Biography and autobiography, as well as fictional portraits, feed Pleasura with the life of another. This quasi-cannibalistic act does for the reader or viewer what true cannibals intend by eating parts of the victim: to gain power by absorbing powers the victim had and which are thought to be lodged in certain organs. Whereas cannibalism fails in its intention, art does not. And the reader/viewer is in fact able to be increased in terms of knowledge, point of view, even wisdom perhaps, by his "ingestion" of the particular work of art, of the life or essence of the thing portrayed.

Art, through its subject matter, can also ignite the pent-up Pleasura in a destructive way. The destructive artistic release of the pent-up energy of the confined Pleasura, e.g., through appeals to the "blood," through submission to the "beast within" (the potential of unrestrained Pleasura desire for gratification), etc., is the artful loosening of its unfettered forces: such are the appeals to tribe and race in Richard Wagner, for example, and such is the appeal to the brute in pornography and incitement to racial hatred, all of which may be transcribed into words, art, or music by competent artists.

In contrast, when the forces of the Pleasura are restrained and channeled constructively by the process of the arts, there is a capability to realize potential for self-realization while at the same time providing the necessary release of claustrophobic energy. The searing works of El Greco shriek aloud, illuminate, and finally offer the viewer (especially his contemporaries) release through catharsis. The works of Michelangelo illuminate the interested viewer, confirming external feelings of an innate knowledge of the beautiful.

The negative imposition of the Pleasura upon its external environment can only be effected belligerently. The unrestrained force of the Pleasura directed externally through the various shadings and gradations of the Pleasura spectrum becomes a force for destruction against the external environment in all its relevant manifestations. Fueled by Wagnerian music, Nazi storm troopers found Pleasura and achievement in acts of barbarism and cruel aggression.

This pent-up claustrophobic Pleasura energy can be seen as a constant dynamic in terms of the interacting elements of the human situation. At one time it can be viewed as passive, dormant, and potential only as in a stick of dynamite that has not been ignited; at another time it is the actualization of that potential, the unfettered explosion outward of the Pleasura in all its energy. The stick of dynamite has exploded.

That pent-up energy is always there awaiting the first opportunity to relieve its contained pressure notwithstanding how long or how successful the dominating, controlling force upon it has been. The pressure is always there like a quantity of explosive powder of the most infernal magnitude, its effects being potentially of exquisite destructiveness.

We are not concerned about the question of the control of the ignition of that explosive: rather, the point being made is that its perpetual potential (and the adjective "perpetual" must be stressed) is the fact in issue. It does not matter for how many eons the potential may have lain (or may in the future lay) dormant: given the necessary prevailing conditions, that potential will, on a perpetual basis, be able to be actualized. It does not matter that the potential has partially or substantially been actualized on occasion; it is not thereby used up as if it were a limited quantity. Rather, it continues to grow and build up in a steady state. Concerning this there must be no illusions, ever.

Proceeding further with the metaphor of the explosive, one could conceive of diluting its potential intensity by a process of controlled release of energy. However, such release must not be part of an accelerated process of ignition for the remainder still stored up, or the opposite end is achieved. That is, the controlled Pleasura being released must not be of such a nature, e.g., "blood" provocations, as to be in itself, upon release, one of the necessary prevailing circumstances to further actualize Pleasura negatively. Thus the Czar Nicholas, in trying to offset the Pleasura stream of the Russian masses, encouraged pogroms that led to further bloodshed and embitterment.

Pleasura-control of its own negative aspects in a positive (constructive) sense can be a windfall to Realitas as a control aid. Methods of positive control of Pleasura release include liberal and universal education. In the turbulence of the Middle Ages this fact was recognized by two monarchs who benefited their realms by being great educators: Charlemagne and Alfred the Great. In the end, the benefits to unity and stability, especially in Charlemagne's realm, were tangible.

Necessary prevailing circumstances for democracies and republics include universal liberal education and free (though judicious) dissemination of literature and speech (judicious in the sense of being non-"negative Pleasura"). The Romans lacked these things: powerful though Rome was, it degenerated from a republic, with all of its concomitant potential, to a monarchical and imperial system. It must be said, however, that any institution or process with the prefix "liberal," must be carefully looked at because liberalism is a double-edged sword: on the one hand, it is the necessary vehicle for the phenomena manifesting positive Pleasura, those things of the upward spiral of humanization. But on the other hand, the "liberal" designation is a tried-and-true false flag for negative Pleasura under which it can camouflage its true nature and interest. Today one sees the bizarre spectacle of liberal protection afforded to pornography and race hate under the much abused banner of "civil liberties." The abusers of this formerly hallowed concept have brought the words into public disapprobation and disrepute.

5

The Human Group as a Human Mind

Although there are areas of casual overlap between the forces of Realitas and those of Pleasura in terms of sharing of the essential elements, in the main those elements are most closely associated with and fundamental to Pleasura. They represent the significant elements constituting the necessary prevailing circumstances required to actualize the Pleasura into its full, explosive reality. It is Pleasura that approximates the id and a review of Freud's* description of the id is revealing also about the volatile and explosive (as well as creative) psychological nature of the Pleasura. Freud sees the id as "the dark inaccessible part of our personality; . . . most of that is of a negative character and can be described only as a contrast to the ego." It is "a chaos, a cauldron full of seething excitations . . . it is filled with energy reaching it from the instincts . . . contrary impulses exist side by side without cancelling out each other . . . instinctual cathexes seeking discharge. . . ."

It is not amiss to follow through with Freud's observations of the ego to enlighten us on our path to understanding Pleasura's dialectical confrontation with the Realitas. "The ego . . . is . . . [a] portion of the id . . . it has taken on the task of representing the external world to the id. . . . In that way it has dethroned the pleasure principle which dominates the course of events in the id without any restriction and has replaced it by the reality principle which promises more certainty and greater success."† It must be remembered that for the purposes of our work

---

*Sigmund Freud, *New Introductory Lectures in Psychoanalysis,* The Pelican Freud Library, Vol. 2, Penguin Books, 1975, trans. by James Strachey, p. 105.

†Ibid., p. 107. See also Freud: *The Ego and the Id,* 1923.

Freud's definitions of id and ego are not conclusive for our understanding of Pleasura and Realitas.

An organized society of human beings, from the most rudimentary to the most sophisticated, is a reflection of the human mind with its corollary, the human personality. Freud is quite explicit on the point in terms of comparing the individual to civilization when he says that "the development of civilization is a special process comparable to the normal maturation of the individual."* The organic whole of the group, so to speak, is much the same as an individual human mind and personality, molded and shaped by the same sorts of influences that mold and shape the individual human being. And, as with the human being, depending upon the relative stability or lack of it, the group's reaction to external stimuli will be, as with the human individual mind and personality, colored by the relative stability or instability of the group as a psyche.

Pre-World War I France and post-World War I Germany shared some of the same group psychological reactions. Taking both groups as if they were minds and personalities, we find that France suffered hurt and humiliation by the Prussians in the loss of the Franco-Prussian War and the loss of the provinces of Alsace and Lorraine. This humiliation had to be borne by the national French psyche, one of fragility regarding matters of its "honor," national pride, and the like. Its traditions since Napoleon had been aspirations of greatness and an innate sense of its prime place in human history as an overall victor. In this regard the psychological constitution of France was one in ascendancy of Pleasura manifested in a national frame of mind analogous to that of the "man of action" seeking and prepared to test his strength in the outside world. To this sensitive ego came the humiliation of the Franco-Prussian defeat and the loss of the two provinces that spurred it on to a position of overbearing hardness in its approach to German reparations and to "terms" with a defeated Germany after the Armistice.

Post-World War I Germany was in much the same fragile-ego state as prewar France. With a "man of action"† ego dating from Frederick the Great and reinforced by Kaiser Wilhelm in the post-Bismarck period, it saw itself in defeat as betrayed on all sides. That is, its mood was transformed by the defeat from one of pride and enormous self-esteem to one of humiliation and paranoia: i.e., Germany didn't really lose, it was sold out. With the seeds of desire for vengeance sown into a paranoid mental state, and aided and abetted externally by the harsh econom-

---

*Sigmund Freud, *Civilization and Its Discontents,* in Freud, the Standard Edition, W. W. Norton and Company, 1989, p. 52.

†*Civilization and Its Discontents,* p. 35.

ically damaging terms of surrender, Germany was in fact a seething, bot-
tled-up cauldron of negative Pleasura waiting for a Hitler to come along
and pry open the lid. In a sense, one can say that the story here is one
of Germany's Pleasura inflamed by Hitler's inflamed Pleasura, resulting
in a sense of flow of history channeled by the forces of Pleasura.

Group mental "stability" or its converse, is here referred to in a very
general sense. The group is taken to be an analogy of a human being
and mind, and the group's assessable mental state is indicated and de-
duced from its representative significant behavior and thinking. In this
work, the behavioral evidence is taken in a *prima facie* manner from its
"historical" record. Nowhere do we pretend to make any sort of authoritative psychoanalytic investigation of the "minds" of nations or groups.
Rather, we proceed on the premise that society, as a reflection of the
human psyche, is open to informed observations and conclusions, especially in a philosophical sense. A caveat would be that supporting data
are reasonably expected and this work tries, though not exhaustively, to
provide it.

Again, we do not intend to delve heavily into the psychological phenomena which are attributes of the human mental situation. However,
they must occasionally and of necessity be touched upon and alluded to
where some explanation may be forthcoming to understand why in our
opinion a certain state of affairs represents a potentiality and why another state of affairs represents a necessary prevailing circumstance to
another potentiality, and so on. Further, this work does not pretend to
be an expert evaluation of the mental phenomena to which it refers. It
offers no apologies for presuming upon the domain of psychiatry in its
theorizing in that no less an authority than Freud himself seems to rec-
ommend its usage to those who are interested. In volume 1 of his *Introductory Lectures* Freud says that "on account of its profundity regarding
its hypotheses and the comprehensiveness of its connections, psychoanalysis deserves a place in the interest of every educated person."*

A group that requires aid in attaining the necessaries of life is a group
in the most basic (and appeasable) state of Pleasura. It is a group looking for a leader, one man or his sometime equivalent in "the many" such
as a committee or a group within the group. This leader-person is a necessary condition for actualizing the Pleasura.

In the century after the fall of Carthage, Rome's economic stability
underwent a roller-coaster ride on its general way down. To compound
the injury, politicians reached new depths of conniving and corruption

---

Civilization and Its Discontents, p. 53.

in the game of the few running up huge riches and political benefits to the detriment of the "many." The masses were cajoled, tricked, cheated, and oppressed by a small number of greedy and shortsighted knights and senators.

The masses' Pleasura was up, and on numerous occasions their kindled discontent found one or more leaders, some of whom, like the Scipios, were high-principled exemplary individuals, but most were common opportunists who sought personal gain and power from their leadership efforts. Notwithstanding the qualities of the individuals concerned, it was the very leadership role they all individually filled that was a necessary prevailing circumstance for the manifestation of the various insurrection movements. One essential necessary prevailing circumstance for the forceful (ranging to violent) realization of discontented Pleasura is the presence of a popular leader.

That Pleasura arising in a time of need (e.g., survival necessity) seeks an outlet through the expedient of a strong leader is demonstrated in the hierarchical power systems of feudalism. In the sixth to eighth centuries the history of western Europe was one of crime, disorder, and disarray, a time of Pleasura survival-need. It was an era of lawlessness, lack of administration, and insecurity. Weaker men and groups searched for alliances with strong "protector" Realitas leaders. This process continued up the feudal ladder, where the Realitas "desire-to-be-ruled" side flowed on as through a series of small waterways joining up with greater ones that in turn do the same and so on till a river is formed.

In the first quarter of the sixteenth century India was likewise in an unsettled state: lacking cohesiveness, universal order, law, and regulation. The land was characterized by embattled divisiveness. The "desire-to-be ruled" side of the Realitas impulse was manifest: it was a land awaiting a strong leader. It proved to be the opportunity for the Mongol Baber, a descendant of Genghis Khan and Timur, to exploit his own Pleasura and conquer India from the Punjab to Bengal (an area conquered by his ancestor Timur a century before). A group in Pleasura suffering a leadership vacuum is a group seeking to submit to such rule, and until the vacuum is filled, the particular group is ineffective as a unit in securing its aims.

The foregoing premise is itself a paradox: in the requirement and seeking of a "leader," the Pleasura group is thereby inviting yet another confinement, another Realitas rule. To disguise the fact (self-deception being the real opiate of the masses), the leader and the group clothe the leader in all the raiment of Pleasura. He is a "son of the people," a "blood brother," a father image, but imbued with the Pleasura of the group; his persona symbolizes that Pleasura. After the French Revolution, its first consul, Napoleon, though a provincial from Corsica, came nevertheless to symbolize the French revolutionary spirit through the heroic image in which he enveloped himself and was enveloped by others. In his profession of carrying the French ideals and its glory to the world, Napoleon came by proxy to represent the French masses. France, in a Pleasura mood to expand throughout the external world in a sweep of conquest, had found its Pleasura symbol, its necessary—and in his case, able—leader (at least for a time). In so doing, France followed its impulse both to be governed and to be governed by a strong leader.

During the course of the French Revolution, the masses already had their "leaders," different leaders, leaders embodying the Pleasura of revolution, overthrow of a strangling and insolvent economic regime, factors that in themselves were prodding necessary prevailing conditions stirring up the seething masses' Pleasura. Men like Robespierre vocalized the mass principles of the Pleasura of unrest, dissatisfaction, and erupting energy. With these "leaders," the anti-Realitas forces of Pleasura were on the move.

Returning to the question of the necessaries of life, the most basic and essential part of Pleasura is the requirement for the satisfactions of the needs of life: hunger, warmth, shelter, clothing, security from harm, etc. The group is awaiting someone or something to supply those needs. Just like an ordinary human being down on his luck, out of work, hungry, and so on, the group members will follow and work for the man who employs them, their "benefactor." If that benefactor bestows upon them apparent kindness and removes from them the essential pressing human needs, then if they are any kind of human beings at all, they will look upon their benefactor as a friend and champion: they will pledge their loyalty and fidelity. And if that benefactor is of their "blood" perchance, they will likely follow him to the death. As we have earlier remarked, "He who feeds me, leads me." And by extension, "He who doesn't feed me, will not long lead me." But further still: "He who doesn't feed me, deceives me."

Now, lest we become starry-eyed about human group fidelity, it should be remembered that the human group is, at whatever its level of progression, not unlike the human individual. Therefore it is susceptible to two major shortcomings with respect to its benefactors: forgetfulness and a low interest threshold. In terms of the former, the group, like the human individual who has just come out of hardship and privation to receive the necessaries of life, soon tends to forget the hardships and privation, no matter how difficult and trying that former state may have been. The group comfortably slips into its new, relieved state as if it had always been so.

That being the case, the second factor comes into play, namely, a low level of interest. The Romans, alert to this, followed bread with circuses. The individual, and in turn the human group, must be entertained. Time lies heavily on the hand and head. When he has his needs to preoccupy him, then, although unhappily so, he is nonetheless occupied. When those needs are satisfied, he becomes bored. At that point he turns to the questions of those things he desires, rather than those things he needs. The matter of adequate clothing is replaced by the question of fashionable clothing; the matter of adequate food is replaced by the considerations of appetizing food. And so on.

It is at this stage that the individual, or the group, as the case may be, is in a state where the potential for the destructive negative phase of Pleasura can be actualized, given the proper circumstances.

If the individual is basically stable, he may be able to channel his Pleasura into paths that will increase its opportunities to satisfy his desires in life, and so he will enhance his employment or his career: invent new ideas, become involved in the arts; or, failing all these, he may just substitute daydreaming and remain in his lackluster state of having the necessaries but not those additional things he desires, provided he continues to obtain those necessaries by continued employment with dignity (the requirement of his basic Pleasura need for self-esteem). The individual may be basically "stable" inasmuch as the self-survival portion of his Pleasura predominates in strength over the aggressive and destructive parts. This would explain the voluntary submission of the malevolent instincts to the more positive outlets of pent-up Pleasura energy. The problem for society is that these more positive outlets—generally the esthetic ones—are less dynamic that the negative ones. In Freud's words, "Instinctual passions are stronger than reasonable interests."*

The unstable individual, however, may try the constructive areas, and if he is not successful, he will not be content to remain in an unsatisfied state, insofar as his desires are concerned. He will be quick to blame the confining environment. He may resort to crime, thus turning against individuals and property in his environment. Depending upon the degree of his instability, his crime will be more or less violent. (By "instability" we are generally speaking of the state of mind that, for whatever reasons, is more susceptible to the call of negative Pleasura in its extremes.) In addition we would include the traditional categories of instabilities in terms of recognized neuroses and psychoses.

Stable individuals would normally seek a constructive outlet for their claustrophobic energies insofar as their desires are concerned or by the

---

*Civilization and Its Discontents, p. 69.

unsatisfactory form of daydreaming or inward brooding introspection. Unsatisfactory though they may be, these inward implosions of Pleasura energy are outlets for the claustrophobic energy. Nietzsche saw these inward flowing thrusts of energy as a form of instability. He thought the inward "attack" replaced the natural, and presumably healthy, outward attack of aggression, which itself has been shackled and removed by Christianity. The inner "attack" of the man upon himself was manifested in what Nietzsche saw as degenerative, namely, conscience and its cousin, remorse.

Unstable individuals, in proportion to their degrees of instability, allow their claustrophobic Pleasura energy to explode outward. In unstable groups, there are reliable signposts that indicate the road that the society is taking in the direction of such catastrophic eruptions.

Negative Pleasura phenomena, in terms of both quality and quantity, are undisciplined and unfettered, the pressure cooker with the lid blowing or blown off. One of the barometers of Negative Pleasura is the alien-as-target: (a) internal and (b) external.

The Alien Internal is perceived and/or actual. The Alien Internal-as-target is the tantalizing raw meat for the hungry tiger, but it is never enough. Unlike real meat, it is siren-like, making the voracious appetite of the loosed Pleasura even greater. It is like the thirsty man who drinks salt water. It is the dreamed-of prey deep within the heart of the unsleeping Pleasura hunger. It is the perceived alien intruder usurping both territory and blood, at the same time challenging and fomenting the blind wrath of the Pleasura.

Therefore the Alien Internal is the first and best target of the Pleasura, having been perceived in the first instance of import to the Pleasura as the threat and intruder to its two most sacrosanct areas, blood and territory. The Alien is not of the "blood," and it is crowding the Pleasura even more by "intruding" into the compressing environment. This intrusion by "nonblood" is resented because it accelerates the claustrophobic pressure (in turn increasing proportionately the force within that screams for release).

The Alien Internal target is the litmus paper of Pleasura danger, whether actual or potential. The acute form is the "similar" Alien target, the "Alien-not-so-perceived"—i.e., in all respects but blood he is often similar to the rest of the group. This form of Pleasura attack can be diagnosed as acute; so intense is the Pleasura rage that it strikes out even where great effort is required. In other words, where similarities outnumber dissimilarities in the object of rage, notwithstanding that Pleasura, except in this instance, chooses the easiest path, like a rampant wildfire or a flood. Where it is prepared to undergo difficulties and even delay to reach its target, its fire has been stoked to ultra-white heat.

Deviation from the "easiest" course in the first instance, the instance of first explosion of destructive, all-encompassing Pleasura fury, comes about because of the enormity of the destructive force stored up. Here its quantity and force is sufficient to channel its own surging stream backward and around to encircle a prey within. Thus the Nazis required Jewish citizens to wear yellow stars to be able to "see" them. A force of destructive Pleasura of that size and consequence imparts, again relatively speaking, the direst of consequences for the group itself as well as the environment. In the first stage, the group will lacerate itself from within, eviscerating its own spirit of self-realization and rendering it helpless before a newer and even more stringent claustrophobic environment. Again, we need only turn to the example of Nazi Germany in the 1930s. In the second stage, it will erupt upon the external environment, seeking to ravage, destroy, and engulf it. Once more we turn to Nazi Germany and its external predations for *Lebensraum* ("living space"), commencing with Czechoslovakia, Austria, Poland, and others. Thus the Alien Internal is the great litmus test detecting potential catastrophic consequences for both group and environment.

As to the Alien External, here we include dissimilar aliens internal to the environment, and aliens—either similar or dissimilar—external to the environment. This Pleasura thrust, which is in the first instance outward rather than inward, requires significantly less effort than in the case of similar Aliens Internal. The former does not have the latter's degree of relative danger (i.e., targeting similar Aliens Internal). At the start it is yet open to channeling wherein reason and logic based on reason's self-survival premises participate as part of the channeling force. Time and adequate argument may yet prevail here by appealing to the most basic instincts of the Pleasura in question through reasoning with it, as in demonstrating by sanctions and show of force that its outward-thrusting ambitions can only result in its self-destruction or leave it, at best, struggling for survival. To illustrate, there are any number of instances wherein international mediation and persuasion have succeeded in halting potential belligerency from advancing beyond the stage of uttering threatening noises. At the Congress of Berlin (1878) war seemed imminent if the conference were to break up: Disraeli warned Russia that war would be declared if the conference broke up. At stake was the break-up of the Turkish Empire, which would give Russia an unprecedented opportunity to increase her power and influence in the region, especially regarding conquered Balkan territory emerging as the new state of Bulgaria under Russian sponsorship. The Russians were adamant about obtaining the location of a Turkish garrison, and were in the mood to press their point aggressively. But they were not in the mood to confront England's destructive might in a war. They doubted England's readiness to go to war. Disraeli ordered that his bags be packed and a train obtained to take him from Berlin if the Russians would not submit. His ultimatum worked. The Russians backed down, Bulgaria was reduced in size, and belligerency avoided.

These reasonable persuasive efforts may not work if the degree of external Negative Pleasura unleashed is too great in its passion to be intimidated or persuaded, or if it is on a collision course with blind self-destruction. The latter is usually the case where the Pleasura group has either superseded its Realitas in such quantum of Pleasura energy that Realitas's abilities to communicate external reality and its dangers are transcended. It also applies where the "strong" leader's Pleasura utilizes the group he rules as a tool for his own outward-thrusting Pleasura (his own megalomania, grandiose schemes of conquest, etc.). If his "terror" or charisma over the group outweighs the group's survival Pleasura, he will, in his intoxication, from his own negative outward-thrusting Pleasura be unconvincible by external persuasion (e.g., sanctions), as with Mussolini and his African adventures prior to World War II, or logical arguments. The results can be disastrous for the ruled group, as in the recent case of the Gulf War and Iraq's intransigence in the face of sanctions and international persuasion, reasoning, and mass condemnation.

Other necessary prevailing circumstances to ignite the fuel of Negative Pleasura are nationalism, blood, soil, territory, and all of their corollaries. These are the factors that on the group-level are reflective of or correspond to the factors that predominate on the individual human level in terms of desires requiring gratification.

These subject heads appeal primarily to the "I" or "me" of the group. "I" or "me" is perhaps the core factor of the phenomenon of human Pleasura, either on the group or on the individual level. It is the "I" or the group "we" around which the world revolves. It is the "I ameba" that recognizes nothing except that the external environment about it must submit to and be absorbed by the "I." Psychological factors involving Pleasura as part of the human psyche are only more subtle variations on the basic ameba theme.

The human individual or group in a Pleasura "unrest" state desires that its importance be acknowledged. From the importance of the "I" in the individual human being we can leap to its equivalent in the "group," i.e., the "us." The general "us" is by its nature adversarial to the general "them." The "us" concept, an emotional phenomenon, is a fundamental, elementary, and essentially unifying one. In particular, it is fundamental to the outcropping of Pleasura in its negative state, in the group.

First of all, let us once more reflect upon what we mean here by the "negative state" or the "destructive state" of Pleasura when it refers to a group vis-à-vis its neighbors. The measuring rod here is the integrity of the group's environment. Simply it is that expression of the Pleasura which, relative to the given group's external environment (external things including other groups), is intentionally detrimental to that environment. That is, the aggressive effect upon its neighbors or neighboring environment characterizes that phase of Pleasura designated as negative or destructive: relative to material phenomena of its external environment, Negative Pleasura is a "harmful" phenomenon. Here we arbitrarily label external aggression as negative even though the motivation of the aggressor state or group may be deemed positive, e.g., from a sincerely perceived need for security.

For an internal meaning of Negative Pleasura, the matter is again simply stated: it is that form of the Pleasura phenomenon that seeks expression in the realm of desire-satisfaction as apart from "necessity" or "needs," the means of such attempts at satisfaction ranging on a spectrum of degree of negativity from minimal to maximal. Proportional to the degree of success in a society of negative impulse to self-gratification is a loosening of the tethers of inhibiting restraints of civilization. These "restraints" originate from the Realitas in the form of categorical "Thou shalt nots" and are the rules and "laws" of the Realitas. These are the inhibitions external to the individual the breach of which represents a crime or injustice in terms of the given Realitas order.

The internal inhibiter emanates from the Realitas itself in the form of indoctrinated morality or quasimorality supportive of the inhibitions of the Realitas. In Freudian psychology the analogy would be to the imposition of conscience and moral inculcations by the super-ego. The internal inhibitions are those emanating from the Positive Pleasura and are representations of morality, one of the ideal goals of Positive Pleasura in conjunction with its end goal of human self-realization. These inhibitions are of the "still small voice" order whispering thunderously the "Thou shalts" and the "Thou shalt nots" into the interminable and endless great silent vaults of the subconscious of the psyche.

As the power of Negative Pleasura of self-gratification begins to rise in a society, in the absence of a corresponding countercheck by the Realitas upon the lid of the Pleasura, the Realitas begins more and more to tolerate public expression and manipulation of the Pleasura's defiance of the inner inhibitions so long as the external Realitas inhibitions are respected. In a tactic of self-survival, the Realitas will incorporate the license involved in breach of the internal inhibitions into "rights" recognized by the Realitas itself so that it does not have to confront this behavior adversarially as law-enforcer versus law-breaker.

Thus in modern Western society we see that from the end of the Second World War, as the economic prosperity begins to wane and as the masses' respect for the Realitas (a respect born of Pleasura identification with government as that of "we the people") declines by its engaging in unpopular acts (high taxation, monetary interference and manipulation resulting in unemployment, the Vietnam War, etc.), the Pleasura of self-gratification notes the opportunity to enlarge itself upon the public stage and seizes it. The Realitas, feeling itself materially and morally weakened, grants greater and greater license to the rising beast that may one day overwhelm it. Realitas puts off its demise that day by throwing Pleasura moral restraints to devour and by sanctioning its self-gratifications as recognized "rights," justifying them and indeed encoding these "rights" legally under the Realitas "thou can" legislation. Thus it is the "right" of movie and TV filmmakers to expose a viewing public, whether or not it so wishes, to acts of sexual self-gratification euphemistically referred to as lovemaking. If the same acts were performed in a public place outside the theater, the participants would, inconsistently, be charged with indecency. But in a public theater acts of indecency are permitted as exercises in freedom of expression. The Realitas submits to the power of the media that can threaten it, and demonstrates its submissiveness by this "liberal" interpretation of freedom of "expression," etc.

All of this granting of respectability, legal status, and recognition to Pleasura self-gratification is rationalized under the great amorphous head of "freedom," a general concept capable of comfortably harboring either viper or lamb under its protective umbrella. Thus the obscene and the loathsome find at law a "freedom" sanctuary together with the conscientious and deserving, a sanctuary recognized by the highest courts in the land. Only the morally indignant are offensive to public sensibility in a land where degeneracy is a virtue.

By comparison to the breakdown of inhibiting Realitas will in a Western democracy, the contrast of the loosening of the tethers of Realitas inhibitions in a totalitarian society is enlightening. Whereas in a Pleasura-oriented "free," democratic society the relaxation of restrictions upon individual liberty by the state encourages greater license-seeking in the name of "freedom," the individual reaction on being freed from a tyranny seems different. Under autocratic rule the individual Pleasura has been repressed, often ruthlessly: it has become forcefully pounded into the desire-to-be ruled portion of Realitas. In a free society the individual Pleasura has been encouraged to develop: given greater latitude, like the camel in the Arab's tent, it encroaches further into license. In the former tyranny, the individual Pleasura, given latitude, retreats (in a Pleasura search for security) to a yearning for the "being ruled" domain once again or unabashedly throws itself into immediate license with which, in its period of indiscriminate Realitas restraint, it has always identified Western "freedom."

In a revealing television interview in the spring of 1992, President Vaclav Havel of Czechoslovakia commented on the phenomenon of newly acquired freedom after many years of totalitarianism. He admitted to insecurity felt by many, himself included. He commented that often one wished "to return to jail" where everything is ordered and set in place. Paradoxically within the new "freedom" the newly free feel unfree; they are confused and frustrated.

In today's Russia many have come to feel "too free" since the advent of *glasnost*. Crime has risen dramatically and the naive conception of many, noncriminals included, is that Western-type "freedom" means the untrammeled right to do whatever one wishes with no state restraints. This is an understandable reaction for a freed Pleasura released from a lifetime of steel-trap authoritarian Realitas control, especially where there has been an enforced vacuum of information regarding the workings of democracy.

There is also a kind of schizophrenic cultural phenomenon that must be worked out by the "newly freed" individuals. In a totalitarian regime the individual must learn to be two people, a public person and an official one (the face his manager and fellow factory workers see) and the other his true face (perhaps) that his family sees at home. With freedom he is free to be one only, but which one? Where does security lie? What is his relationship to be with a new Realitas, a "free" one? What face should he wear?

Inasmuch as the need to survive might appear to approach logical justification for outward aggression upon the environment, the ostensible or (invalidly) proclaimed "need to survive" therefore becomes the great rationale for aggression outward upon the external environment. That is, the probable true cause is generally not relegated as it properly (generally) should be, namely, to the satisfaction of mere desire, a seemingly immoral cause; rather, it is expressed as a matter of need, and in so doing, there can be universal understanding and identification, even if it cannot be condoned. It must be understood that the Pleasura is cunning and extremely skillful in its control of the minds of men, which, after all, is its sole key to freedom. Again we can turn for examples to Nazi Germany and its rationale for external conquest being *Lebensraum,* the apparent need for living space, and not more accurately, desire for empire-building.

The Pleasura in its "I"/"me"-heightened process demands at the very least, "understanding," if not outright approbation. That is, within the framework of human society the Pleasura also seeks approval and wants to be massaged with understanding forgiveness and even sympathy for its acts of aggression. Apart from mere ego-massage, there is also a more practical side to Pleasura's desire for approval. Condemnation brings with it the danger of retaliation by outraged or fearful third-party groups. This could hinder or stop Pleasura's aggressive motion, which it would not consider desirable. Thus, rarely, if ever, in human history does one encounter the exercise of negative Pleasura in terms of aggression upon its external environment without an accompanying rationalization of "need."

Let us again consider the word "right," which was briefly touched upon earlier. At that time we suggested that there are no "natural" rights, just natural expectations. In its defensive efforts at rationalizing and justifying, Negative Pleasura borrows the expression "rights" from the more positive form of Pleasura. Let us examine that incontestable given that humans have rights, which they acquire at birth. These "rights" purportedly create corresponding obligations upon our immediate external environment (our immediate neighbors and contacts) and the external social environment generally. Inasmuch as the concept of "rights" is accompanied by the equal if not more important concept of "obligations," the notion of human rights becomes a powerful weapon for either good or bad. The most important criterion of how the effect will materialize is the nature of the proponent's Pleasura. Positive Pleasura proposes "rights" on both moral and utilitarian grounds. Natural expectations reflect both of these as well.

These "natural expectations" may be reasonable and logical within the context of a rational society, i.e., in a society that can be said to be moving upward and onward toward its self-realization in terms of all of the generally acknowledged and normally positive human values. The accommodation of such expectations in a rational society is therefore done not through grudging "obligation," but through a sense of acceptance, on grounds of reason and humanity, of the premise that such reasonable expectations ought to be reasonably met. The philosopher Immanuel Kant held that when giving a beggar money, the giver should thank the beggar for the opportunity of partially rectifying the moral inequity of disproportionate distribution.

Such natural expectations arise from the need of the human individual to survive physically, and to grow and develop essentially, with the aim of human self-realization in sight. In proportion to the degree of advancement toward "humanization," or self-realization of the human essence is an acceptance of *reasonable* human need and desire expectations, and of the general seeking of ways and means to accommodate them. The justification of nonmoral ends is prudential and "pragmatic" in that such a policy and action will increase the capability of humankind physically and mentally to progress along the road of self-realization. That is, such a policy will result in a greater number of healthy minds in healthy bodies (if all reasonable needs are addressed), thereby increasing the odds in favor of greater numbers of human beings emerging with the potential for advancement along the road to self-realization and with a potential for advancing humanity. We shall have occasion to refer to self-realization later.

The phenomenon of "bonding" is integral to group identity. The strength of group unity is a variable. But in order to be a vessel of Negative Pleasura, a group must be interlocked with a strong unity bond. That is, the group must be adequately unified emotionally so that it parallels a single individual emotionally, an individual governed by his emotions rather than his reason.

   Our species has struggled from earliest times through Pleasura needs (such as survival) and Pleasura desires (such as power) to link ourselves into groups with other humans. From the family to the tribe, the city, the state, and so on, human beings have bonded together fueling mass Pleasura with themes of the group's greatness, which reflect satisfactorily on the individual egos of the group participants, thus establishing a vicious cycle of interdependence based upon mutual Pleasura ego-bolstering. The inevitable negative potential of group bonding with such Pleasura fibers are alienation, war, states of perpetual dissension, and universal anxiety.

   Once a group—with Negative Pleasura potential (be it an old group within a larger group environment or an entirely newly formed group of individuals sharing a common bond such as "blood" and "territory," or political/social unity rationales)—has bonded strongly, then given the necessary prevailing circumstances, the group will manifest Negative Pleasura, which will erupt in an outward thrust of claustrophobic energy.

   In Egyptian civilization, the earliest forms of government were city-states. These, perceiving common interests, combined to form two kingdoms: (a) Lower Egypt (the Nile Delta) and (b) Upper Egypt (to the south). About 3400 B.C.E. Menes, the ruler of the southern state, developed dynastic ideas, and he struck at the northern state, conquering it and commenced the dynastic period of Egypt. (When Alexander the Great added

Egypt to his empire, the thirty-first dynasty came to an end.)* Again, later (ca. 2160 B.C.E.) after several centuries of a loose sort of feudalism, one of the nobles succeeded in founding a new dynasty—the eleventh such ruling family. The dynasty, flexing its muscles with the newly established order and a prosperity that followed, extended the boundaries of Egypt to miles above the second cataract of the Nile and even attempted to conquer Syria.†

At about 2000 B.C.E. the Minoan Cretan culture flowered and demonstrated a harmonious Realitas, with a populace whose Pleasura state was obviously well under control. As evidence that not only was mass necessity satisfied, history shows that desire was also addressed, in this prosperous island, for crafts expanded. There were artisans, masons, ivory cutters—even evidence of wooden lavatory seats with flushing systems was found at Knossos, with further evidence of drains and sewers. This was a fat prize waiting to be taken should the opportunity arrive. On mainland Greece, a wave of Indo-European-speaking people invaded, and unlike the Minoans, they were men of violence. There was a fall in population and reversal of civilization as the Indo-Europeans settled in, not unlike the masses of other Indo-European hordes that permeated the frontiers of the old civilizations. But here in the Aegean Sea, they were the first Greeks—the Myceneans. For some centuries Myceneans developed their Realitas, drawing and building much of their culture from the Minoan and keeping an interested eye on the juicy plum of Crete. The Mycenean Greeks' culture continued to aspire to the ideals of war and attack, as reflected in their art and monuments: the Minoans continued in the opposite direction. Then about the end of the fifteenth century there was a great volcanic explosion on the Isle of Thera. This was the opportunity for action and for satisfaction of the Mycenian covetousness of the Minoans. The mainlanders invaded Crete and seized Knossos. The Myceneans took over the Minoan trading routes, having converted the palace at Knossos into an arsenal to service their own warring needs.‡

By the first century of the Christian era, the Goths (a Teutonic people) had moved out of Scandinavia southeastwardly through Russia, settling in the region between the Don River on the west and the lands east of the Dnieper River. During the third century C.E., they raided the northeastern frontiers of the Roman Empire. Later, two main divisions formed arbitrarily as a result of their geographical locations vis-à-vis the Dnieper

---

*Davies, *An Outline of World History,* 5th ed., Oxford University Press, p. 15.
†Ibid., p. 26.
‡Jack Lindsay, *The Ancient World,* Ebometer Baulis and Sons Ltd., The Trinity Press, London and Worcester.

River: those west of it, in Dacia, became the Visigoths, and those to the east the Ostrogoths. The result was two smaller demographic groups born out of the larger one; each group was ready, able, and willing in their new incarnations as separate and new self-identifying entities to pounce down upon the Roman Empire when the necessary prevailing conditions were right. These conditions arose when the populations of the two peoples began to increase but the weather and vegetation of the fourth century grew drier, giving rise to the need to seek greener pastures.

A further condition goading the Visigoths into action was the threat posed by the Huns of the late fourth century C.E., as a result of which the Visigoths moved into the province of Pannonia* and became a population subject to the Roman Realitas. By now the Visigoths possessed their own individual lore and recognized bonding brought about by the circumstances of the particular territory they had originally settled west of the Dnieper and which had conferred upon them their new, individual identity as "a people." This barbaric nomadic people, sharing a culture that revered plunder, was a natural vessel for Negative Pleasura, the basic fuel simmering since the remembered third-century raids against Rome's northern frontiers. Negative Pleasura, like a shark, is aroused when it smells blood, and this it did when the Roman Empire splintered into the more vulnerable eastern and western empires in 395 C.E.

Earlier, in 378 C.E., the aggressive Visigoths at Adrianople defeated the Romans under Emperor Valens who died in the battle. As a result, they were permitted to settle in Bulgaria and became the first independent barbarian nation in the Roman Empire. Their successes against Rome only whetted a continuing Negative Pleasura appetite for further war and plunder. Under their leader, Alaric, the Visigoths rose up and revolted against the eastern empire and attacked Italy and the western empire in 401 C.E. The Negative Pleasura blood was up and hot and the years 408 and 409 C.E. saw successful sieges of Rome resulting in great ransoms. Then, in 410, the Visigoths succeeded to the pinnacle of their aggressive strivings: they captured and looted the once mighty Rome itself—*Voe Victis.*†

This bit of history is greatly contracted (as historical examples often are) but it shows, very simply, the coming together of a people into a particular group and then, when the necessary circumstances were in place, the group being propelled by Negative Pleasura into outward aggression.

---

*That part of Hungary west of the Danube.

†"Woe to the vanquished," a taunt of Brennus, leader of the Gauls, who sacked Rome, when a question was raised about the method of weighing gold being brought as ransom by Romans.

It should be remembered here again that one of our arbitrary categorizations of Pleasura as negative is the manifestation of outward aggression as opposed to negotiation. This nonvalue labeling pertains even though the Pleasura group manifesting the external aggression may in fact have an objective basis.

The following point must be made: groups that combine because of a common political or social interest may be comprised of different and varied racial, social, and class types. In the absence of the all-powerful "blood," the bonding point of interest must be strong enough to cut across all of these various representations which, in themselves, are bonding factors for their own respective groups.

The Huns, a Mongolian people, were driven off the boundaries of China and made their way into the heart of Europe. They were nomadic, and their common purposes were to drive on, find good grazing lands on which to settle, and to attack and plunder on the way when the occasion was right. These could be called overall Pleasura objectives. Being nomadic, the Huns were, by their nature, tolerant and prone to assimilation with new and conquered peoples. We find that notwithstanding their specific racial and cultural differences, they nevertheless mixed with non-Mongolian races excited by the same Pleasura goals, including Nordic and nonnomadic people, absorbing all of them into the larger group with its Pleasura objectives. This massive group of Huns included the diverse racial and cultural intermixtures; it moved and acted as one entity, a common Pleasura spear aimed at common Pleasura targets.

For another example, we turn once more to Nazi Germany and the Waffen S.S. corps. By war's end, Nazi policies of racial purity were subordinated to practical logistical needs and the racially "elite" Waffen S.S. took in participants from other European nations (many of whom the Nazis had designated as "lower" racial types, e.g., Slavs). These diverse groups were all to a degree Pleasura-bonded and united by the hypnotic "superman" elitism symbolized by the two crooked Ss of the S.S. insignia, and by the allure of Brutus's mastery and conquest, as well as mundane Pleasura goals such as revenge against neighbors.

One constant, universally reliable bonding is that of potential or actual economic benefit to the majority type among the diverse types asked to combine into one group. An example is the European Common Market (the regional trade bloc grouping we spoke of earlier) which, for a common and universal set of potential factual economic benefits, brings together a variety of groups and nations, including various blood and racial types, into one union acknowledged as a "market." So long as the eco-

nomic benefits or their compelling potentialities are there, the union will
remain: in their absence, the cause d'etre as well as the binding factor
of the union will have been extinguished.

As an aside at this point, due to the diversity of ethnic and even "blood"
types in Europe, a united states of Europe in the true sense of one united
country or domain is highly unlikely. There is no one universal common
Pleasura-binding factor stronger than the individual ethnic and national
Pleasuras of the various nations of Europe. The closest approximation
to such a state of unity is the European Common Market, invoking as
it does the universally attractive "economic benefit" feature. But that is
a limited and pragmatic association of states: the appeal to Pleasura here
is not to a "blood"-like loyalty to that united economic market entity that
supersedes the individual national Pleasuras of the member states. Rather,
it is an appeal to the basic individual "needs" Pleasuras themselves as
the cement that holds the economic union together. Quite simply, the basic
premise of the union is that each member state will prosper economically
far more because of participation in the union. Further there is the
"exclusiveness" appeal, i.e., the appeal to the superiority syndrome that
accompanies any "exclusive" organization of individuals or of groups.

At this point one must address the phenomenon of Pleasura-inspired
adversity among ethnic groups of the same general blood, e.g., Slavic.
At first blush this seems a contradiction in terms. The *Oxford Compact
Dictionary* defines ethnic as "pertaining to race." And yet, if we use the
Slavic example, it would seem that ethnic Slavs fighting themselves represent a racial, blood house divided against itself. This flies in the face of
our proposition that "blood" is the great Pleasura unifier. The present
ethnic warring between Serbs and Croatians in the former Yugoslavia is
a bitter and bloody spectacle: history is recording the blood-letting and
agony of war in Bosnia-Herzegovina. The irony is that the participants
look upon their individual identities as the "blood," not on their pan-
Slavic blood association. The "blood" as the great invoker of Negative
Pleasura is an idea, after all: there is no biological behavioral determinism based upon the blood constituency. There is no Slavic (or Teutonic,
or Mediterranean, etc.) instinct in the blood, only the Pleasura and Realitas spectrums. It is most difficult for the Pleasura to invoke fervor in
favor of the general: the human mind finds difficulty in grouping with
the abstract. It must have a particular. The particular component, "ethnic race" within the more general race, is therefore the "blood" that counts.
Thus Serb can fight Croat and so on, for the ethnic (in terms of the
particular, inclusive racial group) is the "blood" that fires the Pleasura.
Should a situation arise where the entire Teuton "race" or Mediterranean

"race" were to rise up against the whole Slavic "race" then the fire would be stirred in the blood of every Slav, and Serb and Croatian would fight side by side as true brothers of the blood against the common threat.

We have not yet addressed "exclusiveness" as a Pleasura phenomenon; this might be the appropriate moment. Artificially imposed "exclusiveness" i.e., as apart from "blood"-ties, etc., is the social phenomenon parallel to the fundamental "appeal-to-the-blood" Pleasura condition: For example: exclusive social clubs (e.g., country and golf clubs), arcane semi-religious and ritualistic associations, wherein the individual ethnic and blood factors of the participants are superseded by an overall binder of appeal to superiority. Thus, in a typical "Gentiles-only" social club non-Jewish members of whatever ethnic background join together in an association that appeals directly to their Pleasura in terms of "us" being better than "them." Generally, such organizations desire a further appeal to Pleasura, and since the binding is a social one, the appeal to their Pleasura on that level is more general: i.e., socially "we" are better than (1) non-Gentiles, and (2) other Gentiles as well who are not as important, influential, prosperous, and the like, as "us." In an organization governed by superiority in order for Gentiles to feel superior to other Gentiles it is an acknowledged given that they must all feel superior to non-Gentiles. Superiority, in the final analysis, implies the Pleasura intent and/or desire to bring others into submission and domination. It also implies an underlying Pleasura lack of self-esteem, which seeks to rectify its situation by a posture of elitism.

Territorial groups frequently come together to form associations, federations, and the like, comprised of different ethnic and/or blood interests: such phenomena imply a constructive step in the direction of civilization in their overcoming of basic Pleasuras for a greater good. Civilization is the way-station to self-realization. Since the quality of such complex grouping phenomena is *prima facie* constructive, it is worthwhile examining the factors that seem to lead to such successful unions.

The coming together of different states or groups into meaningful union means that in each case such an act of association must result in a union that is, in its unity, a greater force for appeal to the individual Pleasura of the participants than would be the case if they remained separate. A major unity-binder equivalent to "blood" is territory. But harkening back to the point stated earlier, in order that such a union be successful there must be the absence of superseding blood and/or ethnic appeals. If there isn't, such a union bears latent defects, cracks in its structure, whether visible or not, that will collapse under appropriate stress, breaking up the whole.

The best-known example of such a successful union is the United States of America. In that case there was a coming of the respective colonies into a federal republic within the territory of North America. The members of the newly formed federal republic were not groups of substantially different, contentious, or diverse blood and/or ethnic phenomena.

Though, the colonies comprising the United States of America were individual communities under their own respective (though colonially limited) legislatures, ethnically and blood-wise, the inhabitants of any and all of the states (colonies) were, for the greater part, ethnically and racially the same. The all-inclusive territorial factor was not superseded by the individual blood or ethnicity of any one of the member states as an effort to establish an obstacle to successful unification. Granted, in the case of the American colonies there were sub-ethnic and racial inclusions such as Germans and Scandinavians—but for the most part the ethnic and racial predominance was English and Anglo-Saxon. Differing from that is the present-day undertaking of the coming together of the states of Europe into a federation, states that, unlike the case of the American colonies, are comprised of different ethnic and often blood ties. As we have noted, these participants have potential for overriding individual Pleasuras, which makes the foundation for such a federal system insecure. In the end, such a federation will succeed for as long as the pragmatic short- and long-term benefits (primarily the former, on a continuing basis) pertain. It is difficult to see such a union developing in its members Pleasura equivalent to "blood" invocations that would result in the types of loyalties and ferocious patriotism universally associated with nationalism. Such a federation would seemingly be a constructive step leaning in the direction of positive rather than Negative Pleasura.

However when (or if) advantages of such union fail or falter, then the individual blood and/or ethnic Pleasuras of the member states would, depending on the prevailing circumstances, come to the fore to threaten or disrupt the union. Such is being seen today in eastern Europe, as witnessed by the former Soviet Union and its respective ethnic participants' now successful struggle to break free of that union.

Witness also Yugoslavia, a political union of Serbs and Croats with its absence of overall prevailing practical benefits of union, in the opinion of the minority ethnic group, the Croats, who now press for independence in a continuing bitter and bloody struggle. At the end of World War I, manipulation of the Treaty at Versailles included the formation of Yugoslavia, a combining of Serbs, Croats, and Montenegrins, harkening back to earlier Serbian (and Russian) aspirations for a kingdom of the south Slavs in which Serbia would be preeminent. In today's struggles between Serbs and Croats, the Serbians, still in the Pleasura flush of the idea of a Kingdom of Greater Serbia (one of whose advocates was the young Bosnian Gaurilo Princip who assassinated Archduke Ferdinand) at the outset of World War I, seem motivated to acquire as much territory of the former Yugoslavia as possible before final external intervention.

There is a mutual and longstanding hatred here among the parties based on a number of classic Pleasura issues: differences in religion (Serbia is Greek Orthodox, Croatia Catholic and Muslim), a desire for revenge for past perceived and real injustices, and a recent historical situation of adversarial quality. In World War II, the Croatians chose fascism and allied themselves with Nazi Germany, sending volunteers in quantity to join the Waffen S.S. armies fighting the Allies, with whom Serbia was aligned. These Pleasura issues now supersede and have resulted in break-up of a union that, to the Croats, seemed to favor the majority Serbs and offer no all-prevailing perceived benefit for remaining discontentedly unified.

An interesting phenomenon is also taking place in Canada, a confederation of provinces. Though some of the provinces have practical grievances and occasionally threaten to break away—e.g., the western provinces—only one province, Quebec, has been consistently militant and energetic enough in its program for separation as to constitute a very real and significant threat. It is also the only province primarily of different blood and ethnic background from the rest: it is predominantly French in both aspects (though the earliest "French" settlers in Canada were possibly of Basque origin), whereas the balance of the population of the country is greatly British and mingled European—certainly Anglophones. We can speculate that the likelihood of any other provinces desiring to break away is extremely limited in that not one of them has a like singular blood and/or ethnic individuality equivalent to that of Quebec.

A qualification to the rule of individual Pleasuras superseding that of the whole is the combination of time and distance. With time and separation from the mother-blood and/or ethnic country, the territorial appeal to Pleasura may come to outweigh even the blood Pleasura appeal. This could be termed the "colonial-Pleasura syndrome" and is illustrated by the Greek colonies of Asia Minor. Though these colonies were of the same blood and ethnicity as the inhabitants of mainland Greece, in the Persian wars a number felt a "separateness" from the mainland to the extent that they saw fit to join with Darius and support him and the Persian cause against their fellow Greeks. The United States is also an example in its coming together in revolution against the mother-blood and ethnic country to form the new federal republic entity with its entirely new territorial (and consequent to that) national appeal to Pleasura over and above any former blood and ethnic ties to Britain. Of course, a vast ocean separated the two. An eighteenth-century French economist described colonies as ripening fruits on trees, falling off when ripe. The elements of ripening include time and spatial distance, which reinforce the colony's Pleasura striving for self-reliance and survival. This in turn leads to the pricking of the further Pleasura inclination of self-assertiveness.

On occasion an anomaly (generally shortlived) occurs where Pleasura need not be manifested only by groups of the same social or racial types. On such occasions equally significant results in human history are obtained by groups composed of diverse social and racial types. In the absence of the major Pleasura bonders of "blood," and "territory," lesser replacement Pleasura bonders are usually manifested in social phenomena of limited or short-term duration. This aberration is exemplified in the uprisings of students, a phenomenon that has in the latter part of the twentieth century become widely known thanks to the media coverage, especially that of television.

Examples of student uprisings or confrontations with the authorities include those which occurred sporadically in Korea (most notoriously in conjunction with the 1988 Olympic Games held in Seoul, South Korea) and as well the radical uprisings of students in France and throughout Europe during the turbulence of the 1960s. They coincide with the 1960s protest movements of students in the United States and in particular opposition to the Vietnam war. Examination of these student protests or revolts discloses a formidable unity of joint "leftist" purpose and interest: more significantly, it discloses that all social areas and classes and all racial types are involved so far as those types are represented with any significance within the social environment out of which the students emerge. This association of individuals is a unity of political purpose bridging diverse social classes and ethnic backgrounds.

A political credo can be a great leveler and an interim Pleasura unifier. It is generally centered upon a political belief as to how the whole world should be run, though often starting from some particular territory or nation. This "how the world should be run" is perhaps one of the most attractive appeals to Pleasura, namely, the appeal to power, to the "we" and/or "our" thought, "our" system that presumably will rule all. It is a paradoxical Pleasura headiness; it anticipates a Realitas to come which will be comprised of fellow-believers ("us") and "our" credo.

The appeal to the "will to rule" or, to put it another way, "the will to become the Realitas manifestation" equals in its Pleasura power even "blood" itself in the short term. Nietzsche spoke of the "will to power" though we may interpret it as a will to Realitas, and the "power" spoken of as being that of the Realitas in controlling the Pleasura within the individual. By extension from the individual who is controlling his passions and is thereby becoming something of a "superman," one can see the Nietzschean principle applied to society as well. In such an interpretation, Nietzsche's psychological philosophy here can be seen to antedate the Freudian "ego arising out of id" to control it: as we have earlier noted, the dialectic of ego and id is predated in *The Birth of Tragedy* wherein Nietzsche's dialectic scenario is between an ordering principle that he called the Apollonian and a disordering, irrational one that he termed the Dionysian (after the god of wine Dionysus). The will to power—the will to Realitas—in the Nietzschean view could be seen as the Apollonian drive to subdue the Dionysian. The paradox of student riots, radicalism, and the like, is that the will to power is generally the Pleasura manifestation of the Dionysian, whereas the subject matter of the Power, i.e., that which is to be subdued, is generally the governing Realitas, or the embodiment at least in part of the Apollonian principle.

A paradoxical "replacement Pleasura binder" rallies and conjoins these diverse student groups under the banner of the Left. From the days of the first French legislature to sit after the French Revolution when the group seated on the left of the speaker represented the most radical elements, the "Left" has come to be popularly equated with that which is potentially or actually in a state of radicalism. This radicalism ranges to the extreme of revolt and is representative of a state of incipient Pleasura upheaval, an out-rushing of pent-up claustrophobic energy to disrupt and overthrow the seemingly confining, detested, and unbeneficial (perceived or real) environment. In acknowledgment of the Left's solidarity with and subservience to Pleasura's most basic ideals (positive and negative), the Left's universal banner is the red flag, the flag of blood: the banner is itself an artificial sort of "blood" unifier. Even the Nazis (an initially socialist party) thought it expedient to allow the socialistic red background to remain behind the swastika symbol in the Nazi flag and armbands, no doubt as a handy evocation to a unifying Pleasura.

It is appropriate at this juncture, where the issue of the Left is raised, to address as well the question of socialism inasmuch as the Left and socialism, as ideas, are, in the public mind almost indistinguishable in many ways.

The toilers of humankind have always formed the foundational segments of society, though Marx first drew their attention to the fact that they formed a class. From earliest times this group has harbored a volatile Pleasura incited by need, desire, and unequal treatment (real or perceived) by the group in power. Socialism is but the nineteenth- and twentieth-century manifestations of this continuum of common mass Pleasura. As a root Pleasura phenomenon it has been and is a thing of the Left. Its dialectic remains with the Realitas group in charge, whether that group is the nobility or the capitalists.

After the fall of Carthage and the growth in Rome of great wealth in the hands of the few who comprised the governing cliques or parties, a popular discontent among the masses rumbled in the streets and back alleys of Rome. The common masses were subjected to wide exploitation. Debts and a disorderly monetary system including all their concomitants were igniting factors that from time to time propelled Pleasura upsurges in the form of strikes and insurrections. These were exacerbated by duplicitous scheming politicians bent on promoting the narrow ends of their own individual Pleasuras and those of their cronies and patrons. The end of the Roman republican era is rife with these strikes and uprisings. There were peasant uprisings in the later Roman Empire as well. The discontent that moved the harassed and oppressed mob was a forerunner of that same Pleasura line of manifestations that finds its modern counterpart in socialism.

This flickering, flowing movement of Pleasura erupted at times throughout history in forms of negative extremes. The peasant wars of the fourteenth century were fueled by this Pleasura. The dialectic here was between the Pleasura-incited common, toiling masses, represented primarily by peasants, and the rich clergy landowners and aristocrats, all of whom were part of the Realitas governing classes. John Ball, a priest orator in Kent who preached equality and resentment of the aristocracy to the poor, could have fitted in easily as a fiery nineteenth-century socialist. The seething Pleasura of the impoverished common masses of the time found outlet in his preachings when he spoke about England never being in a right condition until all goods and property would be held in common and until distinctions between gentlemen and common men ceased. He attacked serfdom and questioned the rights of the Realitas privileged group to exploit the masses. That English uprising was quelled by the assassination of the leader of the insurgents Watt Tyler, by a member of the Realitas, the mayor of London in the presence of the then-nominal head of the Realitas, King Richard II himself (1381).

The Pleasura wave found expression earlier in a peasant revolt in Normandy (1000 C.E.) and later in France in 1358 in the "Jacquerie" movement, also a violent manifestation. Here the French peasants, in anticipation of that later revolution, rose throughout the countryside, burning castles and wreaking havoc on the property of the rich. Europe was absorbing this current of Pleasura like a blotter and in the ensuing century it flared up anew in Germany, ignited by economic and religious causes. Between 1532 and 1535 the Anabaptist outbreak led to a temporary installation of a Realitas arising out of the Anabaptist Pleasura, with an attempt at establishing a religious communistic system in Munstor, in Westphalia. These and other uprisings of the fourteenth and fifteenth centuries were the manifestations of pre-socialism, of mass laboring-man Pleasura.

Though the Realitas groups of all the relevant periods utilized adequate terror and cruelty and trod down the flames of the common masses' Pleasura, that Pleasura has never been snuffed out. It catapulted up at the end of the eighteenth century in the French Revolution, erupting from time to time into the first half of the nineteenth century, and finally settling out in the onrushing flow of nineteenth-century socialism. It erupted violently again at the beginning of the twentieth century in Russia, and later on in the middle of this century in Asia.

This ongoing Pleasura stream of mass discontent moved from pure emotion to a certain self-consciousness in the nineteenth century. The socialist movement is a phenomenon of self-awareness, an imposition of an ego by the Pleasura to let it see itself as it was in itself and as it was in relation to the rest of society. This Pleasura, even with its new-found self-awareness, was not immune from negative manifestation. Marx appeared on the scene and informed the working masses that they comprised a class. Thus for the first time the vessels of Pleasura could stand apart and see themselves and could configure themselves into the dialectic scenario framed by Marx. Its underlying thesis was that the dialectic can end only one way, violently, by the working class rising up, overthrowing and confiscating the property and rule of the capitalist Realitas class, and, in a word, to itself become the Realitas.

A more benign form was taking expression in the early nineteenth century, springing from the more positive end of the Pleasura spectrum. It was embodied paradoxically in the person of Robert Owen (1771–1858), a member of the wealthy classes comprising part of the upper end of the pyramid of Realitas. He was an industrialist and a wealthy cotton spinner from Manchester, England. In fact, his efforts most probably generated the title "socialism" in the first place.

As a side issue of interest, why would a wealthy Realitas member be altruistic toward the masses of his workers? The cynic would say that it was out of self-Pleasura, to eliminate the wastage of labor caused by intolerable working conditions and circumstances. Another view could well be that this man, a self-made wealthy man at an early age, was, from his own peculiar material and psychological circumstances potentially a manifestation of Positive Pleasura, of humanness and human self-realization. He reformed working conditions in his factories and he improved the relationship and dialogue between employer and employee. He abolished child labor for the very young, improved the sanitation facilities and hygiene of his factories, instituted unemployment pay, established schools for the workers' children, and criticized the excesses and inequities of the manufacturing class of the day. At Manchester and at Lanark he put into practice in his factories all of his teachings and he was instrumental in the passing of the first Factory Act (1819).

The observation to be made here is to note the cause-and-effect pattern vis-à-vis the respective Pleasura potentials exhibited by Owen and Marx. The gross injustices they each saw and recorded stirred them both to action. Both Marx and Owen seem to have been roused by these injustices of the factory system in its exploitation of very young children: in *Capital* Marx recounts in vivid footnote detail the astounding injustices of the English industrial system perpetrated upon little children (and he is writing after the Factory Act). Both men in their own ways were reacting in general to eleventh-century industrial abuses. Owen was moved benevolently to a Pleasura expression of a socialism existing compatibly within a capitalistic Realitas. Marx, however, was stirred to rise up as the spokesman for the violent and negative body of this Pleasura mainstream, no doubt due to his differing psychological and material circumstances and their particular reaction on the Pleasura potential within himself.

A moment should here be taken to address a question of interpretation that might arise in the minds of some; that is, in talking of the Pleasura of the toiling masses, we have been referring to it metaphorically as something "ongoing," as a "wave" and "stream," as "a flickering, flowing movement," etc. The implication in such terminology is that we are referring to some great transcendent thing, some extensive, invisible organism that hovers above humankind, all the while undergoing changes in mood from placid to violent, and that the minds of humans are to it like billions of individual mini-sponges soaking it up into their psyches and reacting in a necessarily uniform manner. That is not the case. The unity is not some mythological external force participating in passive individual minds of men but rather the phenomenon of sameness of basic internal impulse of human minds. That content is a fixed, integral part of our nature; in particular the Pleasura part of it is at any given time either in potential as to any number of possible manifestations or is in fact actualized into one of them.

The individual situations of human minds may uniquely predispose certain individuals toward one area of the spectrum of manifestations rather than another, as in the cases of Owen and Marx, but the substantial general nature of the phenomenon of Pleasura is the same in all human psyches. The apparent and indeed actual unity of mass reaction from time to time is dependent upon the variable of external prevailing circumstances.

It is noteworthy that the potential for Negative Pleasura can be siphoned off by a Realitas sensitive to this need. In the England of Owen, laws prohibiting combinations to control prices forced the numerous masses of working men into secret societies or ostensible social organizations in order to fix and maintain for themselves minimum prices on the one commodity they all sold, their labor. Such organizations and the work they did were fertile soil for the manifesting of the familiar aspects of Negative Pleasura: violence, intimidation, and the like. Thus workers who would not join in or abide by agreements with them were termed "black-legs" and violently treated. If left alone, this negative element might in due course have assumed greater and greater proportions and power, eventually significantly influencing the contemporary social-psychological dialectic in England.

The English Parliament, however, headed this negative possibility off at the pass by granting to workers in 1824 the right to collective bargaining, resulting in the development of trade unions. The destructive hot steam of Negative Pleasura was siphoned off: the Pleasura of the workers was recognized and allowed to crystallize out its ego, one that would stand between that mass Pleasura and the reality of life in this contemporary English, capitalist environment of the time. There the new Pleasura creature known as trade unionism was formed, a phenomenon that was and is by its nature less negative than the mainstream body of socialism. That is, whereas socialism intends to change the entire system, trade unionism is content to live within the system as it is, preoccupied only with its own individual Pleasura concerns of need and desire.

The subtle difference in the natures of the two phenomena have not precluded the tribunes of more radical socialism from trying to merge the two systems, and not it should be said, without some measure of success. The headiness of Negative Pleasura, it should be remembered, is always a tantalizing beckoning lure to the remainder of the body of Pleasura. Marx tried to meld the two into one. In his dialectic scenario the melded two are embodied in the one class of the proletariat whose destiny he proclaimed was to combat the capitalists internationally and violently seize their capital by means of revolution.

In his romantic naivete Marx believed that a new utopian common-ownership of the means of production and of property would bring an idyllic state of bliss wherein human beings would voluntarily work to the best of their capabilities, would be content simply to have their needs satisfied, and would use their leisure to improve their minds and talents (almost à la human self-realization). He forgot or was unaware of the unswerving and unchanging nature of Pleasura forever taking refuge in our hearts and minds: personal gain, personal advantage, personal profit, these are the things to which individual Pleasuras cling with ferocious tenacity. That is not to say that these things represent good values, but simply that human selfishness comprises reality and that human selflessness is the exception to the rule. There can be no greater danger to the future and survival of the human race—if such is indeed a good or necessary goal—than a naive disregard of the realities of permanent psychological fixtures within the mass of human minds, especially that of Pleasura. It is always there, it always has been there, it forever always will be there.

English Fabian socialism and its German counterpart "Revisionism" followed the current of Owen-type socialism. Marx's firebrand dialectic scenario held the greater appeal for the emotions and Pleasuras of the working class and he therefore succeeded in forming the first International League of Workers. However, not understanding the entrenched nature of Pleasura, with its priority invocations of blood and territory, he believed that when organized, the workers of the world would only fight the capitalists of the world, that they would transfer their Pleasura goals to the idealistic aspirations of international state capitalism and collective ownership. In the First and Second World Wars the socialists of the European countries did not come together in a great combat against all the capitalists, but they did come together in two such military struggles against each other. They of course succumbed to the patriotic calls of their respective countries, to "territory," "fatherland," "people," "blood," and so on, as they always will when the chips are down.

Returning to the former Soviet Union example, one can take the point of view that the Pleasura, which was resident in the common toiling masses of the Russian people, was invoked in 1917 by the Communist ideals. (To do so is dangerously simplistic in that by skillful organization of the "few," the Bolsheviks took control of the "many." However, that "many" did finally succumb to Bolshevism through terror and value indoctrination and did not rebel against it until recently.) If one takes that point of view, the break-up of the Soviet Union must be seen, as we observed earlier, as due to the Pleasura of those same masses now taking up residence within the goals and philosophy of the capitalist system. The Soviet system has been disrupted and is in the process of being replaced with something new: but something "old" will remain, namely, the vast body of Pleasura resident in the psyche of the masses.

To the extent of Pleasura's universal "permanence," the aspirants to the Realitases of humankind would be well disposed not to throw out the baby with the bath water. Socialism has no special class claim to the addressing of our basic needs: Prince Otto von Bismarck, Prussian chancellor from 1871 to 1890, recognized this when he, a nobleman and the Realitas incarnate, introduced socialist-type benefits for the German toilers. The authoritarian Bismarck was astute enough to understand that with Germany's massive and sudden industrialization new needs would arise in the masses of workers. If not addressed, these needs could give rise to confrontations. "Conservative men and socialist measures is a potent political formula."* Thus one sees late nineteenth-century German workers benefiting from contributory old-age pensions, unemployment insurance benefits, and the like, all of which were harbingers of modern twentieth-century social benefits. But his philosophy was one of expedience, not of humanness: his sops thrown to satisfy mass Pleasura were to maintain work efficiency and progress. When more humane and liberal social considerations arose, he made his own judgment that mass Pleasura of necessity had been adequately placated to efficiently grease the wheels of production, and he would go no further. In the Westphalian coal miners' dispute of 1889, in opposition to the Kaiser's wishes, Bismarck would not give in to liberal demands and was prepared, as the prime moving Realitas force, to employ terror and send in troops.

In a sense Adolf Hitler can be seen as a direct successor to these policies of Bismarck and the Kaiser as well in his realistic recognition of the need to appease the basic Pleasura of the working classes. In *Mein Kampf,* the latter-day manifestation of extreme negative Pleasura, Hitler clearly sees its workings and prerequisite conditions. He recognizes that because of arbitrary refusal by the "bourgeoisie" (his familiarity and casual lapsing into the use of such a Marxian term quite possibly denotes an influence and indebtedness he would not wish to have acknowledged) to meet justified humane demands, many workers were driven out of the less abrasive trade unions into more (adversarially inclined) political activity. In this point of view he is more a follower of the Kaiser than of Bismarck. But in relation to the Realitas of the German Empire, Hitler is certainly in the camp of Bismarck. The latter, however, as the Realitas leader, was satisfied with the united Germany itself as the empire (apart from the ill-fated anemic attempt at African colonization, which resulted in more than twenty-five thousand German subjects occupying lands—deserts—vaster than all of Germany). Hitler had far greater ambitions. Hitler and the Nazi Realitas participated in a Pleasura drive to subjugate all of Europe and Russia as the new and greater German empire (the Third Reich).

---

*Crick, *In Defense of Politics*, p. 130.

The basic needs of Pleasura are a continuing concern for any totalitarian Realitas governing body that wants to keep the lid on the ever-simmering cauldron of Pleasura within its geopolitical boundaries. It is suicidal for any Realitas group—especially a totalitarian one—to disregard the needs and aspirations of the Pleasura, unless it is prepared to rule through terror and coercion. The latter stratagem must eventually run out of both will and substance, for prolonged terror drains the vital resources of a country.

Diverting resources to maintain terror, which is, in the main, capitally unproductive, must in the end drain and emasculate the body of a country and the power of the governing Realitas. A modern-day example is that of North Korea where jail gulags and labor camps must continually be maintained at great national cost to provide for the incarceration of an estimated 150,000 political prisoners, and where armed forces unproductively account for the consumption of 24 percent of the country's annual gross national product. One could also talk of the country's eight billion dollar debt, its lack of essential raw materials resulting in nonoperation of a major portion of the country's factories, and so on. These are not necessarily the products of inadequate leadership: rather they are the inevitable results of prolonged maintenance of terror and its supporting system of resources, which, in the long run, must bankrupt a society by its profligacy. The fatal flaw of all autocracies is inefficient distribution of resources.

This mortal defect flies in the face of the Pleasura rationale for autocracy, efficiency. When in the long run a long-lasting autocracy inevitably succumbs to economic reality, a suppressed population (whose Pleasura of freedom-seeking has been capped both by terror and an overriding Pleasura argument of efficiency of economics) will experience a rising Pleasura of indignation and rebellion in its gorge. One need only look once again at the remnants of the former Soviet Union: generally the new states have energetically discarded the former communist system to its core with a vehemence that bespeaks volumes in terms of mass discontent.

The two main socialist philosophies of the late nineteenth and early twentieth centuries can be gauged in terms of their lasting influence and their own permanence in light of how they dealt with the reality of Pleasura. Communism scores lowest because its pure aim was to totally abolish property in favor of common ownership. Socialism, on the other hand, scores "less worst" in that it recognized a category of things as being capable of private ownership: it stressed that only certain things such as land, transit, distribution, and all natural production phenomena should be the property of the state. It also recognized that within these parameters the citizenry should be protected as to personal freedom.

Both communism and socialism failed to confront economic survival, the most basic need-cry of Pleasura: both, but especially the former, have not mastered that degree of efficiency in the distribution of goods that satisfies basic needs and begins to address universal desires. There are still great gaps between social theory and practice. The fly in the ointment of socialist administration of wealth and resources is that such is managed by human beings subject to all the narrow considerations of individual human Pleasura. If a man will get paid for slacking as well as working, why work? As Dr. Samuel Johnson put it, "We would all be indolent if we could"; under socialism we can. Again, having said all of this, reason once more counters with the caveat of not throwing out the baby with the bath water.

Radicalism is a true erupting-Pleasura type of phenomenon struggling to burst out of its claustrophobic bonds, and, like Samson, to bring down the pillars of the temple of environment.

In true extreme Pleasura form, radical extremism (and this can be of either left or right wings) forgets that, in its destruction-bent euphoria, in bringing down the temple it is necessary, like Samson, to also perish in the general ruins. But in speaking of radical extremism, we are talking of a phenomenon of Negative Pleasura (though it should be noted that in America all radicalism is considered political extremism).

An argument can be made that radicalism itself, as a general claustrophobic Pleasura phenomenon, has its own positive to negative spectrum (in relation to the range of goals from social reform to total social destruction). Radicalism and romanticism in the general sense are more than kindred spirits, they are the closest of kin. Radicalism is a term originating from the Latin *radix,* or root, and aims at the Romantic Pleasura ideal of absolute cleansing of the Realitas at its very core, of all of its iniquities. In this sense—what we will call its "Pure" sense—one can say it is reformist in nature: in its extreme (and here we mean "negative" extreme) it is destructive in nature. In both of these senses radicalism echoes the spectrum of its very substance, Pleasura, though perhaps radical extremism may be seen more as a negative extension of the spectrum of radicalism than the extreme end of radicalism's negative spectrum.

In its euphoric naivete radicalism shares with romanticism the notion that humankind may be unclothed of its many layers of Negative Pleasura—of greed, inequity, high-handedness, sadism, etc.—like the peeling of an orange, and thus a pure, virgin form of society can be achieved.

But the clothes will not come off: over many eons they have solidified into a kind of second skin.

Their perpetual and encumbering pressure must therefore be acknowledged and addressed in terms of humanity's problem of adaptation to civilized existence carrying with it, as it always does, this excess baggage.

The naive, romantic notion that influences radicalism is the Rousseau idea that humankind is basically and generally good: this is a very wide and indeed positive form of Pleasura appeal, almost ethereal in comparison to the rest of the inhabitants of the House of Pleasura. Society, as seen here in Rousseau-like terms, is the corrupter of humanity. Thus, in the romantic view, the corruption does not come from within but from without: that is naive. Naivete is the fatal flaw of romanticism and romantic philosophy. The "corruption" potentials within are not placed there from without but are only aided and abetted by the corruption from without as they actualize within the individual. To give Rousseau's ideas their due, however, it must be said that they contain a partial grain of truth: insofar as the corruption from within is in great part at least potential, it therefore requires for its manifestation the agency of external circumstances, a range of which can be ascribed to the external social environment including but not limited to the institutions of civilization. One might say that the naivete ascribable to radicalism is evidenced by its implicit premise that human ideals are achievable: they are not. Ideals are unachievable goals that serve to inspire the determined traveler along a wearisome, uphill road. Success with regard to human behavior and achievement is measured in terms of the linear progression along that road. Paradoxically, success is based on how close one comes to achieving that unattainable goal.

Socialism then, in that it wishes to change society, is a Pleasura-Radicalism phenomenon, its methods determining it as radical or radical extreme (in the latter case, a manifestation of Negative Pleasura). That is, in the former case, socialism as a radical phenomenon seeks, like Owenism, to change society by reform. Socialism as a manifestation of radical extremism, on the other hand, seeks not so much to change society as to overthrow it violently and start anew with a new set of rules, as with Marxism. In that regard, socialism as a form of radical extremism is a vehicle for Negative Pleasura.

At this point certain criteria must be refreshed in our minds. Negativity is so designated from a purely human chauvinistic viewpoint: that is, from this perspective, the good rests in the peaceful, harmonious interinvolvement of humans in society (or civilization) with society itself progressing linearly, as it were, toward the absolute goal of human self-realization.

We have arbitrarily categorized as negative that form of Pleasura which seeks, without objective justification (e.g., self-defense), to perpetrate aggressive action upon the external environment and, in particular, a relatively noninjurious Realitas order and upon other human beings who are innocent and noninjurious. In other words, acts that manifest the intent of the brute. These admittedly are very broad criteria but in their broadness they catch the essence of the meaning.

There is no time here for a detailed examination of objective tests and standards of the stated criteria. Certain truths are here taken as self-evident: for example, that it is not a good thing to punch one's neighbor in the face just for the fun of it. At the same time, it is admitted that historical examples illustrate cases where reform could not be effected upon an objectively bad Realitas and resorting to force was justified. It should be added that the examples being historical and therefore anecdotal are *prima facie* cases where violent Pleasura uprisings seemed valid, as in the French and American revolutions. Therefore, the label of Negative Pleasura is qualified in this regard. If we were alive at the time of the historical events to make our own judgment, other more reasonable methods might indeed have been seen to be open as an alternative, ones perhaps not recorded or intuited by the contemporary historians upon whose accounts we rely.

Political extremism must be relegated to being a subhead of Negative Pleasura, one of its variably manifested phenomena. Pleasura, like a driving swollen river, will seek out any channel that is open to its surging flood. The intent of Pleasura is analogous to that of existence itself, namely, to manifest itself in the particular whenever and wherever possible, bringing in its wake Negative Pleasura as part of itself.

Negative Pleasura seeks out casual accomplices: for example, war-bent governments are occasionally unwitting instruments. With the high exaltation and euphoria that Pleasura-on-the-move provides, these governments succumb to its lure of destructiveness in the belief that it will justify the virtue of their political credo. That elevates them above morality to a new conscience, one whispered into their ear by Pleasura, a "conscience" that sanctions the destructive and the immoral as it replaces their normal sense of guilt with a newfound euphoria of nobility of purpose and participation. Youth especially are prone to this type of heroic opiate because of their inexperience of life and because of the intransigence inherent in the omniscience of immaturity. It must be remembered here that we are talking about ends of aggression, which are in the main dictated by Negative Pleasura motives—e.g., group aggrandizement, territorial acquisition, and the like—and not, for example, cases of preempting mad dictators intent on nuclear destruction (where such preempting is indeed reasonably possible and reasonably called for in the circumstances).

The locomotive of extremism does not work according to a schedule of stopping at way stations. By its nature, it is continually gaining momentum and, to arrive at a destination, those aboard must risk throwing themselves off. If they are lucky they will

(1) arrive intact,

(2) arrive at their intended particular political destination and not bypass it.

A paradox of socialism is that, notwithstanding its being a system of belief on the Left, it must nevertheless come to terms with an internal confrontation of both principles of Pleasura. Its leftist credo aims at a replacement of the existing Realitas capitalist regime and society and is instigated and impelled by one of two ways of thinking:

(1) a genuine Positive Pleasura humane desire for humanity's betterment by replacement of the present political and economic system: in effect, a sincere aim at freedom from the perceived undue constraint, inequity, and unfairness of the Realitas environment; or

(2) a Negative Pleasura feeling of "ressentiment" in the sense that Nietszche expressed it. That is, a general envy, detestation, and hatred of the present system because of its perceived success, and certainly because of the reality of the fact of its being the Realitas: the governing (ruling) factor. Part of this reasoning is the desire to replace the system just because it is there. This feeling is manifested in radical extremism.

Another paradox of socialism is that its leftist goals aim at "freedom" from the old "tyranny." "Freedom" here is a kind of euphemism for "take over" from the old Realitas "tyranny." But what is this new "freedom" if achieved? It is a political and economic system of paternalism, wherein the state owns and controls all natural resources, communications, major industries, and more: the responsibility for all things of importance will rest with the state and not with individuals. In other words, the practical end of socialism—especially the radical or extreme variety—is the replacement of one perceived restricting regime with another that is considerably more restrictive and possesses far greater potential for political and economic repression. The source of this repression would be the state with

all of its coercive resources (e.g., the military). Though a benignly inten-
tioned phenomenon, socialism is the potential vehicle for tyranny, a Realitas phenomenon not intended by its more moderate advocates. This is
how nazism found its fundamental socialist structure to be an expedient
road to its eventual despotic Realitas.

Perhaps a more realistic problem in terms of a socialist Realitas is
that the state is a bad landlord. As in the observation of Joseph Chamberlain earlier concerning empires, namely, that like prudent landlords they
must improve their real estate, socialist states often lack this incentive.
A socialist state is an organization in a holding pattern, holding the assets it has received for its constituents, like a trustee. The mere holding
of these assets is in itself the practical end aimed for in the Pleasura of
the movement. The socialist state therefore lacks the Pleasura incentives
of a beneficial owner: the property belongs to someone else, though that
"someone else" is in theory the people. Included with the real estate is
the business associated with it, government and, to an extent, economic
control. Again, these are not assets in which the state has a beneficial
interest. A trustee under sound instructions and financed by a responsible beneficial, owner will generally carry out those instructions or be removed. Who is to remove the trustee here? And who is to give the instructions and provide the financing? The people. But "the people," as
the great reservoir of Pleasura, are concerned about their own self-interests
first. In a capitalist society these are addressed, but in a socialist one the
interests of the state—the trustee—are addressed, and the interests of the
people are indirectly addressed through the trustee. In a practical sense,
both finances and instructions are weak and, in the end, so is real estate
and business, both of which are ripe for a fall into serious decline.

The foregoing is the paradoxical political (potential) outcome of socialism. That is, the socialist Pleasura, thrusting ahead as it does, fueled
on dreams of economic liberation for the individual from the bonds of
an "unfair," "inequitable," and "restrictive" capitalist Realitas may, if it
succeeds in its aims, arrive at the very opposite in terms of freedom and
economic liberation. If evidence is needed, all one need look at is the
frantic expediting of the metamorphosis of the former Soviet Union to
a free-market economy. At the root of the turmoil is a desire of the majority of the masses in a paroxysm of Pleasura to throw off the environmental "shackles" of socialism, which proved in many respects to be even more
limiting than czarist Russia.

Reality teaches that society has been, is now, and will be hereafter
comprised of Pleasura-dominated human beings. Pleasura, the two-edged
sword (destructive passion and the desire for human advance and self-
realization), will always tempt humans to taste the apple of exploitation-

of-freedom (for self-gain at the expense of others). "Freedom," if properly utilized and not debased into license, may lead to the emergence of a greater number of individuals progressing along the road to self-realization. But the caveat is evident: Pleasura tends to misuse freedom for negative rather than positive ends.

For Pleasura to rise up against the Realitas, accompanying the unifying factors of Negative Pleasura there must also be a collateral lack of fear of the external environment. This can be artificially muffled or masked by Negative Pleasura emotion-culling such as the inspiring of resentment and by invocations of nationalism, "blood," and the like. This Negative Pleasura emotion-rousing can dim reason, normal prudence, and discretion, even in the case of overwhelming and unbeatable Realitas superiority in strength and numbers. Pleasura in this mode is the egoless id.

At this point, an observation is in order about coercion as a child of terror and a tool of the Realitas. Coercion's appeal to fear is the paradoxical use of a Pleasura property by the Realitas. Once the external environment—let us say the governing or Realitas group—no longer can or chooses to impose fear upon another group, if that other has the necessary factors present for manifestation of Negative Pleasura, it will occur with the predictable results. The obvious cases are those of autocracies, but even democracies are not exempt, for what happens if police authority or presence is even temporarily removed or absent, as in looting by rioters? Perhaps, though, "sanction of law" is more accurate in the case of democracies than the word "coercion."

Again, we turn to eastern Europe where such a phenomenon has been exhibited during the late 1980s. The Soviet Union, battered and drained of resources, lost its will (more so than its ability) to continue its imposition of terror over its own people; it "influenced" territories and groups, and in so doing had to come to grips with the Pleasura self-determination phenomena within its circle of dominion. Poland, Czechoslovakia, Hungary, and East Germany broke away. Then came the attempts by the Soviet Republics to be independent and free: Georgia, Armenia, Lithuania, Estonia, etc. The element of hatred of the Soviet Realitas was more or less present in all the Soviet satellites and republics: bravado and daring in the face of superior police and army forces characterized confrontations in Poland and Czechoslovakia and in the very heartland of Mother Russia. It culminated with Boris Yeltsin standing on a tank to address supporters during an attempted coup by former Realitas adherents. Further, it was a violent and tragic student confrontation with superior police forces in Czechoslovakia that acted as the straw that broke the camel's back, leading directly on to Czech independence. Combined with these sorts of events came the accelerated diminution of Soviet terror leading to a (well-founded) lack of fear by the Pleasura-inspired masses. This intermingled with the long-smouldering hatred of the deprived, ruled masses, sparked by desperate economic wants. Combative Pleasuras of former satellites erupted at every opportunity.

No group is immune from these powerful forces of Negative Pleasura once the salient factors are present. A prudent Realitas society will therefore take heed of these factors and of their volatility in terms of social stability. It will also recognize that, like a volcano, there may have been no eruptions in long memory, nevertheless the explosive potential is always latent deep down, just waiting for the right conditions to be activated. Only a grossly naive and negligent system of government would overlook or be indifferent to this.

6

Pleasura Unifying Factors

The recognizable presence of a Pleasura unifying, bonding factor within a group—e.g., "blood"—usually evidences a potential or real state of Negative Pleasura with all of its concomitant and resultant phenomena able to arise.

Of all the unifying factors, the most dynamic is that of "blood." It speaks to the most basic and fundamental stuff of life itself, and when used in the context of a particular "blood" group its unifying effects are overwhelming, even euphoric to the group as it undermines reasonableness.

The basic premise of "blood" arguments is the heady stuff of Pleasura, namely, "My blood is the best blood." The blood of Pleasura has mystical properties making it more than just blood. It has intrinisic values that are too great even to be measured, and can in the end only be described by the statement: "Of all the bloods on the face of the earth, of all the liquids on the face of the earth, of all the red corpuscles and platelets and white corpuscles, and so on, the particular combination comprising *our* blood is the most precious, so that it is unthinkable that even one drop should be wasted. Every drop is hallowed and should be worshipped as sacred. That blood of which we in our group are all made, binds us together mystically in an arcane fraternity of the blood and raises us all up on high, even our lowest ones, so that all other creatures find a place somewhere below us, sorting out their own ranks somehow to their own satisfaction and to our noble indifference. We dare not even bleed, so precious . . . so precious. . . ." In Nazi Germany, in spite of the Nazi program to exterminate the Jewish populations of Europe, the Third Reich hesitated and often refused to execute citizens of mixed Jewish-German blood because of the presence, in those persons, of German blood.

This factor, when influential in terms of a particular group's Negative Pleasura, is the most lethal because it is the most rudimentary, the most primitive. As such, it vibrates in harmony with the most brutish types of acts in terms of aggression, actions most closely identified with the situation of human outrages one would most likely attribute to the primitive "lack of conscience." If vestiges of conscience remain as a result of the civilizing process, they are stilled by the "blood's" rationalization of "necessity." But in truth, "necessity" is superseded and not even requisite as a cause ofttimes when the "blood" can be invoked. Other rationalizations are injustice, danger—and here the "blood" calls on Pleasura's ally, paranoia, for support—and so on.

For examples of "blood" paranoia one need only review the lengthy historical catalogue of this phenomenon, which parades partly under the title of anti-Semitism. Especially apt, of course, is the example of Nazi Germany and its anti-Jewish policies and laws. Again the Third Reich's policies illustrate blood paranoia, as witness Nazi policy toward the Slavic peoples. Inasmuch as the Slavs were considered of inferior blood, it was decided that these people would thenceforth be treated as inferior races, little better than slaves after the war. Nazi policy in 1939 after the invasion of Poland became akin to that of the ancient Spartans toward their helot slaves; they were to be leaderless and kept emasculated in terms of power. The Nazis instituted a program of extermination of Polish nobility, army and civic leaders, and other persons of position. All potential for leadership (and the Pleasura organization) of this "lesser" race was to be removed. This was a problem that the S.S. had to overcome with its death-camp operatives, but the S.S. succeeded. Loud was Himmler's praise for these people and the necessary "service" they were rendering to the Fatherland.

For the Spartans the "inferior" helots were deemed to be slaves by their very natures (Aristotle thought also that slaves were so by their natures) and kept severely reined in like captive animals, not humans. When helots distinguished themselves in battle fighting for the Spartans, the most heroic of them were taken and rewarded by execution lest the helots acquire inflated ideas of their own worth. (The Spartan Pleasura was also one of "self-survival," fearing danger of uprising should potential able helot leaders not be executed.)

Inasmuch as the incantation of "blood" is in effect a stripping-away of all of the multifold layers of the civilizing process to the bare bones of the raw and savage state, those groups in a state of Negative Pleasura whose primal call is to the "blood" have carte blanche to Pleasura's palace of pleasure, sadism, and cruelty of the most exquisite orders.

The closer one gets to the rudimentary and primitive invocation, the greater the success of response from the group or individual in a state of Negative Pleasura. This response is to a greater or lesser degree a potential in every human being. It is a latent repository of every group. It lies just below the surface of the civilized skin like a tense violin-string waiting anxiously but patiently to be set in vibration and to scream out its own special cry.

"Territory" addresses a primitive and basic human-as-animal situation. With other animals, territory is a true necessity of life inasmuch as certain territory only holds enough forage for a specific individual or group of individuals. Therefore, such territory is vigorously defended out of necessity. It is still a fundamental subject matter of the psychological content of human-as-animal Pleasura with direct input to the negative portion of its spectrum.

Are the impulses by which other animals react a form of preprogramming? Cannot the argument be put forward that humanity also is preprogrammed somehow as to its potential instinctive impulses and as to when and how these impulses are triggered? However, if so, is humanity not purely determined? Not necessarily, if this line of reasoning is to be pursued, and this line of thought is certainly not novel. Innate knowledge and ideas have long been a subject of enlightened speculation from the time of Plato.

Animals have no understanding or capability of voluntary control of their preprogramming. Humanity, on the other hand, is capable of an overriding understanding of those phenomena (whether programmed or not) that drive, compel, and impel it, and those causes that spring the impulses. To a great extent, if that knowledge is coupled with a positive willing, those "determined" phenomena can be voluntarily controlled and manipulated. But will is in the last analysis the process of decision between two or more choices. Enter the problem of how that decision is made. Is it "over and above" any manifested impulses and their influence? If not, is reason strong enough to overcome the impulse influence? Enter the problem of a concept of regression of will back to some ideal non-impulse-influenced decision amounting to 'will'. Presumably, in such an impulse-sterile atmosphere reason then would decide on its own accord. Can there be an act of will, outside the will, to regress back the will to the point beyond impulse where reason only will influence decision or originating will? Or does this whole line of reasoning turn into an infinite regression of wills and thus lead us nowhere? These thoughts are touched upon to indicate the complexity of the problem of will in its relation to impulse. This writer prefers the common-sense approach, i.e., at some point the judgment or decision is made. Since decisions are continually made, there may be a universal plateau of decision-making in the thought impulse process (excluding unnatural influences on decisions such as insanity, drugs, alcohol). This plateau can be called, for our purposes here, the (universal) responsibility level. Presumably one can posit the insinuation of reason into the process here, thereby justifying the epithet "responsibility." In other words, there is a point where the individual stands over and apart from the scales of decision-making, weighed down as they are by impulse, and throws something down on one of those scales to tip the balance: this is the act of will, the ultimate act of responsibility. This is the point at which, if the choice is a loaded one, i.e., impulse-influenced itself, the individual knows it in light of reason, and makes the choice nevertheless as a judgment of personal preference: here the individual consciously reaches out either to positive or negative Pleasura as a matter of choice: this is the realm of responsibility. As to infinite regression, it could be argued that the final choosing is itself influenced and therefore not voluntary, and therefore one must go back further, and so on. Common sense, the great natural arbiter, says however, that at the responsibility plateau, one need regress back no further for if there *is* influence here, it is no longer, at this stage, of such overpowering compulsion as to negate voluntariness. The impulse-influence at this plateau, though existing, is of a sufficiently diluted (by reason) nature that the compulsion for a wrong choice, as it were, can be overcome by reason. Here the responsibility for the decision is not so much the influence of impulse as the free-choice of the individual. This is will in action.

But this choice itself is the individual's own choice, his own thing, relating to his judgment and to his own estimation of his capabilities to judge, to master events by his personal judgment. Therefore it then becomes an element of significance to his Pleasura in the same realm of importance as pride, for example. Thus Pleasura clamps its teeth down hard upon the decision and holds fast to it until the desired outcome occurs. The interested onlooker sees the tenacity and persistence of Pleasura here and describes it as the individual's strength of will.

Knowledge and understanding of the nature of a preprogrammed phenomenon is what makes the great difference in the issue of determinism: understanding the compelling phenomenon is equivalent to being able to control it. But that controlling power, to be complete and locked into place, requires the key factor of effort of positive will (or will to the positive) so to do. If power and positive will are together, they act as a formidable bar to the igniting power of any existing relevant necessary prevailing circumstances. This is true of all impulse-igniting phenomena: necessary prevailing conditions to activate the potential in humans, e.g., for Pleasura eruption (both positive as well as negative) are only fully operative in the absence of the combination of understanding *plus* determined will to the contrary. To the degree that this psychological union is present the determining power of the environment is limited.

Returning to the question of territoriality, possibly our forebearers had similar territorial requirements, for hunting or for general food-gathering purposes. Or perhaps the territorial instinct is one, as we have suggested, that is genetically programmed into organic life and is thereby within the human individual as one of the basic instincts. In any event, like "blood," and almost as powerfully invoked, "territory" is also an incitement, along with all of its similar rationalizations, to calling forth Negative Pleasura of the most primitive kind. "Territory" is so similar to "blood" that the invocations to the one can, in most cases, be used for the other. "*Our* territory" is special, is of mystical value above all others binding us of the same "blood" to it. "Our territory" is the most special on earth. Its very soil is of greater value than the substances that comprise soil of any other territory. We are made special by our territory, and not one precious inch of it must be lost or allowed to be taken away, not one stone, not one stick, not one blade of grass, not one earthworm below the surface, not one iota of slime on that earthworm below the surface of "our territory," and so on.

To realize how strong our territorial interest is, try traveling abroad without a passport. The stringency of human borders, the jealous guarding of them by the uniformed representatives of the respective Realitases says to the incoming stranger: this is our territory. You cannot come here except upon our strict sufferance. You are lucky to be here, in *our* territory. Not far removed from all this is the situation relating to the territories of wolves in the wild, which stake out their boundaries with urine sprinkles and woe to the trespasser. The territorial imperative does not diminish valid territorial "necessity" considerations. For example, what mad recklessness would incite any country to open its borders helter-skelter to all and sundry who might be inclined to enter? What brigands or unfortunates with dangerous pestilences (e.g., the plague) could enter under these "liberal" open-border circumstances? With knowledge and understanding of the phenomena that desire to control us one should also come to the fiat that, in controlling them, one must avoid recklessness at all costs.

Sharing the same harmony of the elemental, "territory" and "blood" go hand in hand as potent triggering mechanisms for Negative Pleasura of the most lethal order. These Pleasura twins go forth together into the mists of the morning of dissension, hand-in-hand. They are the pied pipers, followed by a long procession of dancing and cavorting celebrants bearing weapons.

At this juncture, the question of understanding what is meant by "negative" Pleasura raises its head. How does one differentiate? Is there a special "line" or point beyond which one finds constructive or Positive Pleasura, and over the other side of which one discovers Negative Pleasura?

As with all antithetical ideas, there is an imaginary line of division between them. The overstepping by either one or the other to the opponent's side becomes significant only as to the degree. A major incursion would certainly result in the substantial taking on of the qualities of the region incurred. But to be precise about the matter down to the very fine points of distinction as to when the degree of incursion results in the substantial assumption of the qualities comprising the nature of the side trespassed upon would require some exquisite philosophical calculus. For our purpose—indeed for practical purposes—the matter should be dealt with on a commonsense basis.

Let us first take the most obvious cases, those not requiring philosophical sophistication, namely, criminal acts. There is no civilized society that does not designate certain acts as crimes. Most designations as crimes are of universal categorization, such as murder, rape, theft, and assault. These are all universally acknowledged acts of Negative Pleasura, negative in that the Pleasura-gratification of the individual is injurious to the well-being of the group. They are also universally acknowledged as immoral. Thus, the obvious examples of Negative Pleasura are acts categorized by the individual's dedication to self-gratification with regard to any given action as prior to and exclusive of all other considerations.

Perhaps to better understand the psychological realm of wishes, needs, desires, anxieties, and the like, that comprises the varying shades of Pleasura, it would be expedient to once again visualize a spectrum image. Let us commence at the extreme lefthand end of the spectrum: let this be the positive end. This extreme positive end can be designated as morality and self-realization, the absolute qualities of which are unattainable but invested with the quality of the ideal. These are the human ideals, the purest and most constructive Pleasura elements. On the positive end they serve as inspirations; on the negative end, incitements and excitations.

As a digression let's take a moment to look at the use here of the word "ideal." Is it suggested that the human psyche (and subconscious) contains innate information about absolutes and ideals? I concur with the thinking holding that such is the case, and based on that premise it seems to me that human self-realization is capable of being approached. The degree and extent of the nearness achieved is the question for eons to come. The existence of a priori information has been a subject of philosophical debate. Noam Chomsky's inquiries into language suggest innate cognitive foundation-structures upon which diversity of language is founded.*

***Reflections on Language,* Pantheon Books, 1975.

It is not the intention in this work to stray into metaphysical discussions at length; that must await another treatise. Suffice it to say that he who denies either absolutes or their unconscious awareness within the human psyche must deny the basic esthetic of the perfectly round circle. Saint Augustine, following earlier Greek thought, declared that the architect designing an arch does so with the perfect (the absolute) one in mind as a criterion. The human mind has an unconscious understanding of (or perhaps "feeling for") that which consciously is ever a source of difficulty of understanding, namely, absolutes. Humans, not other animals, aspire to straightness in the lines of their dwelling structures and see beauty in symmetry. How are we to judge "straightness" and "symmetry" if the absolute criteria are not already known, albeit unconsciously and latently, in the mind? This has long been debated. In the same manner, innately the human mind has knowledge of that "perfectness" which is the end goal of Positive Pleasura striving. If it did not, why would we applaud a Mother Teresa? Against what other criteria could such people be designated as saintly? If the alternative answer offered is reason, then where does reason get its basic premise, a value premise from which to proceed to the conclusion of saintliness?

Returning to the question of the Pleasura-spectrum, we begin the departure from the purest (the most positive—the ideal) qualities of Pleasura, through the less positive (though still substantially positive) qualities of Pleasura. To use another metaphor, as we depart from the "pure," we travel progressively through the part of the spectrum of "tainted" Pleasura. As we approach the dividing line between negative and positive Pleasura the degree of "taint" becomes increasingly greater until at the dividing line, the prospect of substantial "tainting" has arisen with a resultant change in nature from positive to negative Pleasura (though positive qualities remain, the preponderance is now negative).

Crossing the line, the Pleasura takes on the aspect of the negative, and, conversely, to the progress from the positive ideal to the dividing line the "progress" here is one of increasing negative Pleasura through to the end regions of this portion of the spectrum, which is universal crime of every nature, i.e., absolute crime as part of absolute immorality. This end of the spectrum is pure Negative Pleasura or as may be more readily understood in terms of humankind, evil.

In touching upon "evil" we might assume that now we are entering into the domain of the theological. Not so. The problem is that Pleasura, a self-justifying phenomenon, seeks not to identify itself with the subject matter of reproach. No aggressor has ever admitted its intentions are malevolent, rather that aggressive designs, for example, are based on necessity or lofty motives. The fourth crusade (1202 C.E.) is a case in point.

Though ostensibly motivated by the underlying desire for liberation of the Holy Land from infidel rule and wanton destruction as originally preached by Peter the Hermit, it was in fact a Latin aggressive design upon the Byzantine Empire; no crusaders ever reached the Holy Land. Embarking from Venice in 1202 C.E. under the supposed standard of the crusade principles, it captured Zara and after encamping at Constantinople in 1203, it executed its final objective by taking the city in 1204. Baldwin of Flanders, a Latin, was finally enthroned in Constantinople as emperor.

The question of "evil" touches in part on the intent of the agent: unless insane the man who deliberately sets out to produce Negative Pleasura results can be described as evil, and the resulting ill effects on human beings not having been produced by natural misfortunes can be described as "evil" effects. Our definition of "evil" here is therefore linked to the incursion by the willing mind into the negative ends of the Pleasura spectrum. Definitions of a "willing" mind and delineations of where these negative regions of the spectrum begin for "evil" purposes and questions of how far into the negative end the incursions must go are not here analyzed in detail. As noted earlier, this is a swampland of difficulty. Rather, we take the "easy" route—we prefer to call it once more by the epithet 'the commonsense route'—of general basic human understanding. Notwithstanding the sophistication of "freedom"-hugging defenders of modern "evils" (Negative Pleasura self-gratifications) such as pornography and violence incitement, "right" and "wrong" are generally instinctively and/or practically understood by all sane persons. The axe-killing of a man by his neighbor would not be excused by anyone as a form of self-expression notwithstanding the axe-murderer's plea that he was "making a statement." (We are here assuming, of course, that in spite of the outrageousness of the plea, we are not dealing with an insane individual.)

By arbitrarily categorizing Negative Pleasura ends as "evil" we are not attempting to stray into ethics, though the underlying ethical implications are there. Rather, we are dealing with the utilitarian, prudential, and the pragmatic. If it is accepted that Pleasura is an immutable factor of the human psyche and that Negative Pleasura is an invariable part of its spectrum, and if it is accepted that "good" is so described in human (including human self-realization) terms, and if finally it is conceded that manifestations of Negative Pleasura are invariably (historically) "bad" in terms of results to humanity, then the conclusion is irresistible. "Evil," in human terms, is identifiable with Negative Pleasura phenomena.

We are not treating the important subject of evil trivially by not proceeding further to examine and comment on it. To do so would require a fuller and more comprehensive treatment than we can provide here.

We seek here only to clarify the guidelines within our thesis as it pertains to Negative Pleasura for the reader's benefit. Let us return then to the question of the Pleasura spectrum.

The "Spectrum" of Pleasura

Positive Pleasura   *Negative Pleasura*
(The ideals of absolute and   (Evil)
  human self-realization)

(Dividing Line)

```
----                          .                              ----
---_____X     .                              ----
---_____. _____Y            ----
---              X ___. _____     ----
---        X _____. _____   ----
---                           .    Y_____ ----
```

From the spectrum image we see that "purity" resides only at the extreme ends of the continuum. The nature of the phenomenon of any given point in the spectrum takes on its substantial coloration and its degree, as it were, from its relative proximity to the end of the spectrum closest to it. We can therefore analyze a Pleasura phenomenon's nature in relation to the side of the spectrum to which it is proximate: its qualities, if examined judiciously and objectively, should be capable of identification in terms of remoteness or proximateness from an end of the spectrum thereby allowing us to judge the degree of "positive" or "negative" nature.

As an example, let us create a hypothetical situation. Let us conceive of an actor who is performing in a play designed to illustrate to the audience the essence and nature of a murder, a portrayal of a Raskolnikov, if you will. Let us say that he begins to be more and more intrigued in a tantalized way with his character so that he begins to depict the character sympathetically with the aim in mind of making him—a monster—attractive to the audience for the reason that the act of murder has now become attractive to the actor. We could now say that the actor has traversed the dividing line between Positive and Negative Pleasura.

Now, if the actor begins to emulate in his private life the characteristics and ways of the character he is portraying on stage, we can see that the actor has crossed the line into the negative. If he makes the subject of murder attractive by way of argument, persuading others, vilifying murder victims and rationalizing murder as justifiable, he is progressing further toward the absolute negative end of the spectrum. And if, finally, persuaded by his own arguments, he tries to emulate the murder he portrays nightly on stage by actually committing murder, then he has taken a giant step toward the absolute negative end of the spectrum, getting as close to that end as is humanly possible.

This approach may seem, at first blush, too abstruse and abstract, too "unscientific" in its method to be relevant. It is not so. Our examination here deals with human nature and behaviorial reaction which is, in the end, not subject to precise scientific criteria. And far from abstract, the phenomenon of human action is, both in its intent (often hard to discover) and its results (easy to ascertain), quite concrete and tangible.

Negative Pleasura recoils from the prospect of its recognition for with that recognition comes the possibility of its control and restraint. It reacts with the self-defense method of ridicule, for that which is ludicrous cannot be taken seriously. Thus, moral terms such as "good" and "evil"—especially the latter—automatically click the element of derision into place when individual Negative Pleasura is strong and seeks to prevail. "You talk of 'evil'?" derides the individual in the sway of Negative Pleasura. "Is this a religious crusade?" In this way the propositions that threaten Negative Pleasura can be put "into their place." He is aided in this derisive "put-down" by the many abuses historically performed in the name of religion which discredit the motivation and sincerity of religious leaders and enthusiasts. Be that as it may there is evil in the sense outlined above and to shy away from that recognition is to invite domination by the ever-willing and able negative end of the Pleasura spectrum.

7

The Realitas and Further
Negative-Pleasura Considerations

Whereas Pleasura represents the dynamics of the content, the Realitas
Principle is concerned with the dynamics of the containing environment.
As we have observed, using the analogy of id and ego, the Realitas can
be viewed as arising from the Pleasura as the ego does from the id. Like
the ego, the Realitas acts as an intermediary between the Pleasura (the
ideal) and the reality of the outside environment. But it also acts as the
ordering force acting upon the Pleasura and becomes its immediate con-
tainer-like environment, externally enclosing the Pleasura by imposing order upon it.

When we turn to Freud we realize that our analogy to his ego and
id is only partially helpful to us: Freud does not seem to view the Pleasure-
Principle id manifestation as a value-spectrum phenomenon. When he
speaks of the Pleasure Principle he asserts that from the start it decides
the purposes of an individual's life. This tallies with our conception of
the initial and prime area of psychological priority given to the control
of the Pleasura from the start. But Freud sees the entire Pleasure Principle as being constantly at odds with the whole world environment, whereas the more positive aspects of the Pleasura spectrum certainly don't necessarily fall into this category.

Freud ties in the delineation of the ego from the outset as being in-
debted to the Pleasure Principle for the boundary delineation separating
the internal from the external world. That is, the infant learns early to
separate and try to control (by limiting unpleasure and absorbing pleasure) the effects of the external; even in infancy the "external" and "internal" are differentiated. Why would this not also be the case during the

infancy of the human species when our ancestors huddled in caves recognizing a threatening external world? The manifestation of elemental Realitas units emerge when individuals governed by the Pleasura start to form the first rudimentary groups, families. These groups would undoubtedly be governed by the strongest or in some other way the most influential individual(s). The group would have dominance and strength to negotiate with the outside world. The other primates, our more primitive cousins, gorillas and chimpanzees, exhibit this tendency to develop families and other elementary social groupings presumably for survival purposes.

Freud also sees this social grouping arrangement as a pragmatic measure in the battle to obtain survival necessities from nature. He sees it as a civilizing factor, but we must remember Freud's approach to the understanding of civilization as being the means of controlling nature for survival purposes: tilling of the soil and reaping its bounty for the prolongation of human life. Further, to Freud the criterion for civilization's advancement is its progress in control of nature. In our work, however, we go much farther, for we equate the progress of civilization not only with its technological progression but with its position on the road to human self-realization, a Positive-Pleasura end. So in all our conceptions of civilization, from its origins, a Realitas manifestation is encompassed.

A further problem in the Freudian analogy is that Freud seems to use the libido as the umbrella covering for the self-preservation instincts, which he sees as including aggressiveness and hatred, and which we see as negative facets of the Pleasura generally. Freud, in talking of the Pleasura and Realitas principles, does seem to fall into place with the type of reasoning we've been developing when he speaks in *Civilization and Its Discontents* of the Pleasure Principle changing into what he calls "the more modest reality principle"* because of the "influence of the external world."

Another problem with the Freudian approach in terms of our thesis is that Freud compartmentalizes the ego and the id into three divisions, namely, the id, ego, and the super-ego. In our thesis, the super-ego phenomenon representing conscience and guilt feelings would form part of the positive end of the Pleasura spectrum and would not be differentiated in a third and separate psychological segment. This component of Positive Pleasura might be seen to meld in utilitarian fashion with the "realistic-view area" of Pleasura, namely, the survival instinct. In effect it says, "unless we, the components of Pleasura, impose order upon ourselves, we are all doomed." Perhaps here the super-ego considerations conjoin to establish a sort of harmony of the prudential and the moral.

---

*p. 26.

The analogy here is to the American Wild West as seen so often in the movie morality plays. Picture a town rife and rampant with lawlessness, a wide-open frontier town attracting and indeed inviting in the wild and the reckless, the drunkards and debauchers, the gamblers and outlaws. Within the town are the hard core of merchants and tradesmen who are profiting by all the money the "wide-openness" of the town attracts. They close their eyes to the many brawls, assaults, shootings, and notorious goings-on until finally the quantum of wild shooting sprees and fire-setting to buildings threatens the very existence of the town itself, including the hard-core merchants and tradesmen and their families. At this very point where very survival is at stake, law and morality are invoked in the person of a marshal who is elected from their midst or imported, to bring legal and moral order out of chaos, to ensure survival rather than a final conflagration set by some drunken, rioting incendiary.

The components of "conscience and guilt" are tools of the Realitas in its ordering and controlling the Pleasura group. In our Wild-West example, the marshal falls under the jurisdiction of the governing town council as one of its peace officers bringing law and order to the region on behalf of the town. The "Realitas" here is the town establishment, including the town council and its leading citizens. Conscience and guilt represent the limited Janus-like quality of Pleasura: though the dominant part of Pleasura is acquisitiveness, conscience and guilt show another side of the Pleasura equation. Can it be said that there must be some pragmatic explanation for conscience, some survival mechanism to make the idea important to Pleasura (which in its negative extreme is selfishness incarnate)? Or, can an argument be made that Pleasura, in its absolute positive aspect desires human self-realization and implicit in that is morality? Conscience in this light therefore would be equated with apprehension of "unpleasure," at it were, resulting from the deliberate perversion or obstruction of self-realization. The "unpleasure" is a kind of painful remorse: but in order to be painful it can be argued that knowledge of the subjects of self-realization and morality must already be components of the psyche, albeit unconscious, the infringement of whose integrity is painful to the individual.

Although the energy of conscience emerges from and resides in Positive Pleasura, the Realitas gains advantage from it. The Realitas comes to symbolize the external "giver" and "taker away" of this psychic unpleasure through the media of rules, laws, and religion. The Realitas is partially analogous to the concept of the super-ego, though the Realitas performs all of its functions on a conscious-level (unlike the super-ego which is partly unconscious). Therefore, the breach of the society's rules and laws is not only imprudent (because penalties apply) but also somehow immoral. Thus in our Wild-West example, the former riotous drunks and brawlers now find themselves in jail for having breached town ordinances, and as well, looked-down on by those merchants who formerly tolerated them for their custom but now reproach them in court for the damages they caused the town.

Lengthy speculation or comment on this point is not desired. Suffice it to say that we see the phenomena of conscience and guilt as part of Positive Pleasura. Further, notwithstanding the limitless exceptions to the contrary (as exhibited in criminal actions of all sorts), human beings in the main respond to the idea of self-realization in whatever form that idea may be represented to them, most broadly in the concept of "civilization." We are prepared to go one step further and describe human self-realization as the subject of an impulse underlying Positive Pleasura. It is the only Pleasura impulse that *prima facie* seems unselfish, though in reality it strives for that which is constant with the spirit of Pleasura, namely, the acquisition of all things that lie within the limitless ambit of human potentiality. It is this goal, human self-realization, that can be seen as the final cause, the end "good" of man. Aristotle in his *Metaphysics* sees the final cause as an end which is not for the sake of anything else but for the sake of which everything else is.* In this respect, man's end good and goal must be substantially a phenomenon of mystery toward which man, impelled by the force of Positive Pleasura, propels himself in a zig-zag fashion, now advancing, now due to the efforts of Negative Pleasura, stopping or falling back. It is mystery because we have no conscious knowledge of the actualities of the essential composition of this end good: intuition tells us what it is like by means of moral criteria and common sense.

The positive impulse is at constant loggerheads with Negative Pleasura. Later we shall comment on the seemingly ongoing dialectic within Pleasura itself, of Positive versus Negative.

The excesses of unrestrained Negative Pleasura inevitably inspire Pleasura reaction of fear for survival within the consciousness of the Pleasura-manifesting group itself and that of its individuals. It is at this stage that the Realitas desire to be ruled manifests itself within the Pleasura group as a prelude to the instituting of Realitas rule. As with the ego and the justification of its existence by the id, the Realitas is a last-ditch survival mechanism of the Pleasura. In our Wild-West example, at the point the merchants foresee disaster for the unruled town, they organize and elect a town council to govern, which in turn appoints our marshal.

---

*Aristotle, *Metaphysics,* Everyman's Library, London: Dent, 1966, p. 364.

Ingrained in the survival mechanism of the human species is a necessary awareness and fear of the dangers of unrestrained Pleasura. The reluctant reaction is a will to submission, a voluntary or involuntary (but de facto) submission to that which will harness the unrestrained Pleasura, that which will muzzle the maddened tiger for the safety of all, though it means that the ecstatic and wild rides on its back are over, at least temporarily. As a result, the tiger is poked and prodded into the restraining cage of Realitas. Always in the back of Pleasura's mind, however, is the longing to ride the wild tiger again. It should be noted that the ego-like positioning of the Realitas does not exclusively mean that it now treads where none was before: rather, it means that where rampant Pleasura was in the ascendancy, the scales are voluntarily if reluctantly turned in favor of Realitas ascendancy and within this type of context a manifestation of the reality principle in terms of prudential Realitas decisions. In the frontier town, the wild cowboys reluctantly submit to the town's new ordinances, handing in their guns to the marshal when they arrive for a night of revelry. Though they know this new instituted order is in the best interests of the community at large, yet they and their compadres in town still dream of wild and untrammelled carousing, uninhibited by law and order.

For example, circa 390 B.C.E. the Gauls, in a state of Negative Pleasura, moved southward into the Italian peninsula. They rampaged through all of Etruria and sacked Rome itself. Here then was a victorious swarm of humanity in high and intoxicating ascendancy of Negative Pleasura. Admitting the human capability to excess in aggression and concurrent self-gratification, the reality of mortal limitations is always darkly grinning behind the shoulder of the whirling dervish-like warrior in shining but bloodied armor. When he turns to stare into those darkened eye-hollows, it is then that he stops hacking, looting, and raping.

The Gauls' sustenance, both materiel and physical, suffered in the prolonged campaign: seiges were undertaken when they were more used to attacking, charging, and making off. The prolonged campaigning took its toll: dissension and disease no doubt erupted within the ranks of the barbarian conquerors. Mortality strode amongst them casting its long shadow over their camp. The spirit of the hordes retreated to one of ordered Realitas, of simmering down, of dealing with reality in pragmatic terms. They negotiated, accepted a substantial pay-off by the Romans, turned around, and retreated into the northern mists again.

One can begin to understand how destructive or Negative Pleasura can be viewed as itself encompassing a broad spectrum of degree, ranging in terms of the human perspective from the lethal and abominable to the least negative and indeed most positive point in the Pleasura spectrum. Examples of the negative extreme would encompass and range from the most flagrant and abominable criminals to the numerous hordes of the atrocious and ferocious, as for example the reputed rapacious hordes of Attila the Hun through to the Gestapo followers of Adolf Hitler. It would also include murder, rape, willful maiming, and criminal acts against children to name but a few. Examples of the most restrained groups (and here we see a melding into Positive Pleasura) would include passive resistance and self-determination organizations and the confederation or other unification of states through peaceful transition or evolution; as for individuals, the fulfillment of self-desire without resorting to criminal or immoral acts generally accepted as heinous or loathsome.

Examples of the Positive Pleasura sphere, on the other hand, include the altruistic pursuits, selfless devotion to the general goal of betterment of humanity and its furtherance along the road to human self-realization. It counts among its vessels those individuals who themselves have chosen to progress—and are progressing—along that very road. Included are the moral (as apart from the self-seeking prudish): the learners, teachers, and practitioners of the arts that open human minds for the betterment, survival, and self-realization of the entire race. (This is a very general sweep and is not intended as a broad or infallible endorsement either of the occupations named or of those professing them, but a rough guide to the seeking out of some of the pilgrims of self-realization, provided they are sincere. (But how do we test for this quality?)

Whenever I see a person, for example, who has spent his or her life in the profession of teaching handicapped children, there is a stirring within me of admiration and a certain feeling of gratitude on behalf of the whole human race. Whenever I hear or read of physicians dedicating their lives to the improvement or cure of physical or mental ills, not out of a desire for fame or for self-advancement but out of a sincere desire to improve everyone's lot, I cannot help being moved and overcome by an overwhelming sense of gratitude on behalf of all humanity. Whenever I see or hear of those individuals (and again we're not talking of regressive prudes) who brave the tide of ridicule and hatred of those ill-advised misunderstanders of "freedom," to raise the banner of morality against the insidious and destructive forces, I am stirred with a deep respect and appreciation. Is this sense of being stirred and moved a sort of catharsis based on recognizing in them the inner images and knowledge contained within the unconscious Positive-Pleasura part of my psyche? Do I experience the broad euphoric sense of relief at seeing manifested in reality those things I unconsciously "know" to be potentials within Positive Pleasura?

At this juncture, I offer some observations. I have mentioned the stirring within me of gratitude and admiration when I see a teacher of handicapped children and I have queried whether there is in me a sense of catharsis-release and elation. I have suggested that this may in effect be a personal response to recognizing in practical reality the type of unselfishness and dedication to human betterment and improvement that is intuited by me to be an integral part of human nature, and in particular pointing as well to what we can achieve and become in the process of human self-realization. I must reiterate the overwhelming understanding that comes upon me of the handicapped-children's teacher voluntarily diverting his or her life's ways and means from the more attractive Pleasura paths of self-gratification (luxury, etc.) to a Positive-Pleasura dedication of energies to this noble but relatively unrewarding profession. Even in writing this I am unable to truly express my sentiments: I can only approximate them, ringing as they do in a vibration of recognition of intuited essential parts of human nature. It is true that all things are ultimately done or chosen out of "selfish" self-interest, even where the objects of choice are ostensibly unselfish. But the nature of the end choice must of necessity reflect upon the chooser and, since none of us are isolated parts of the whole, upon the essence and nature of humankind itself. Where the choosing is negative, where it is cruel and bestial, there can arise a despair within the human soul at seeing and recognizing this part of our nature. But where the choosing vibrates in harmony with the "end good," then the despair is replaced by an elation mingled with wonder that our choices, necessarily "selfish" in origin, can yet strike like a true arrow into the heart of the positive. These positive manifestations may not be heroic —they may only be on the level of teaching the handicapped—yet the close contemplation of them mysteriously stirs the heart.

Alike with Nietzsche I can recognize in a large, physically strong person a potential neanderthal brute. Unlike Nietzsche, I do not admire the potential brute or the "brutas" or see the "taming" of this person by civilization to be retrogressive for the individual or the human race. Rather, again with a certain naivete perhaps, I feel a sense of appreciation and even admiration that the potential brutishness of this individual is conquered, tamed, and that by this very act of civilized compliance and participation he is progressing along and evidencing the reality of the path to human self-realization. Brute power is voluntarily given up—no small thing—and the person behaves himself.

There is much strength of will needed for the individual or indeed, the species, to choose and progress along this path inasmuch as the barricades of Pleasura bar the way at every spot along the road, particularly wherever the traveler grows weary. The barricades must be thrown down, hurdled, or even lamely walked around. But there is help in traversing and progressing along this high road of species excellence in that there is a compulsion within the species to draw near to the end goal—to the "end good" of which we spoke earlier—which is the completion of this journey, a journey that paradoxically, can never be completed but only progressively continued. Aristotle hinted at this compulsion when he described the soul as being inexorably drawn to its end. The end is the "humanness" part of the human primate species, the germ of which is transported by means of the primate vehicle, the protoplasmic engine to get us there.

Now, in talking of "bettering" the human species, in talking of its improvement in terms of self-realization, in talking about its "perpetuation," are we really just using a euphemism for the unrestrained populating of the earth and is this something viewed as an end in itself? This becomes the dilemma par excellence.

In the first place, the perpetuation of the human species is essential for a practical reason, the law of possibilities: that is, the perpetuation of the species increases the number of positive possibilities, e.g., that relevant individuals will arise to aid humanity in recognizing and voluntarily moving along the path of human self-realization over time, that it will be aided over time in this exercise by the emergence of the requisite leaders and teachers, and so on. But then comes the question of the nature of that perpetuation. The propagation of human life is not a remarkable process in terms of its mechanics: any human male and female can sexually conjoin. In fact, they do so daily by the billions. The problem is that the masses in those geographical areas and in circumstances where the offspring of sexual union look forward to lives of abject poverty— a mere existence if that—are little removed from lower animal forms of life. One has only to look at the groveling masses of India, populating sidewalks and gutters, and one cringes, embarassed at being "human." These wretched, miserable, and unfortunate stations of human life are perpetuated in the millions throughout Asia, Africa, and Central and South America, in areas notorious for recurrent drought and famine. Is this the perpetuation of the human race so earnestly to be desired?

These masses exemplify sheer Pleasura gone wild. Though the Pleasura phenomenon manifested in mindless overpopulation is not negative in the relative sense of external force, nevertheless a violence is still being done— more subtly and in its own way equally devastating—to the possibilities of actualizing human self-realization. For, with numberless masses of the wretched to be cared for in their pathetic circumstances (hunger, disease, lack of shelter)—and this must be done, for human life *is* precious above all else—a great part of our energy and resources must necessarily be diverted to this task. Also, the futility of perpetuating such human wretchedness with no reasonable prospect of anything more positive to be hoped for, in terms of human self-realization, is demoralizing. Such pitiless self-degradation of the human species is a negative prevailing circumstance barring "the species" progress toward self-realization. Logistically, it is also a phenomenon that could undo the human species.

At this point the critic can respond: "Why do you speak of overpopulation as a Negative Pleasura manifestation? That is, implicit in that description is the underlying assumption that blind overpopulating of the planet could spell humanity's doom. But you have earlier conceded that Pleasura propels out of itself the Realitas—like the ego—as a survival measure. Therefore, if in the last analysis Pleasura seeks survival, why should it embark helter-skelter upon an obvious program of self-destruction that it cannot combat?"

The answer again is paradoxical. The paradox of Pleasura's promotion of wild, reckless overpopulation is that it thereby seeks if not its own survival, at least its own continuing power. In its encouragement and carnal stimulation of the masses it thereby ensures the domination of the mediocre and the mean. It is not the fault of these unfortunate numberless offspring that in the main, being undernourished and uneducated and spawned in inhuman conditions, their better potential can never be realized and that the most to which they can attain is mediocrity coupled with a Negative Pleasura-incited desire to further propagate their kind. But these wretched individuals are not being vilified here: rather their situation, inculpable though they themselves may be, is here generally and broadly addressed.

If it seems that because of negative external prevailing conditions (or lack of them) with their resulting failure to realize good potential (or on the other hand, their actualization of negative potentials) that the spilling forth of this portion of humanity is here criticized, it is true. We have not addressed the possibility of negative and deficient genetic traits perpetuated by this indiscriminate and epidemic type of breeding but it is there. The fact is, practical reality must be dealt with in these questions, including the question of the freedom of assembly-line coupling. These are questions to be agonized over, and so they must.

Common sense says that the exponential growth of the human population like ants is self-defeating in terms of progressing to human self-realization. It is impossible to feed, clothe, and medically oversee, let alone educate, the masses in the dizzying numbers that animal-like undisciplined breeding produces. At least with other animals they breed in season. Humans breed at all times, whenever and wherever the opportunity to greedily reproduce manifests itself to the willing and otherwise not incapacitated. Thus the sidewalks of so many cities in underdeveloped countries crawl with hordes of human forms swarming in their numbers like buzzing insects. Is this where the nobility of human potential is housed?

Similarly in the Western world, old welfare generations in need of of welfare and new generations (a modern phenomenon) of street beggars and the permanently impoverished (their numbers greatly augmented by the mentally ill and those addicted to drugs) also extend themselves gleefully to embrace irresponsible self-gratification. The old welfare system is by now a culture, a set of values reinforced by Pleasura both of necessity and of negative self-gratification.

No, the populations of the more economically privileged classes are not here being excluded as some superior, valuable segment of society that deserves perpetuation. Not at all. These individuals are equally subject to the same caveats to overpopulation. It is by the luck of the providential draw (though let us not exclude individual talent and ability) that they have the economic capabilities to address both the necessities of life and educational possibilities. Mostly they are just plain lucky. But we are not here talking of the deserving versus the undeserving: we are talking about the reality of those who are least suited but most disposed to propagate the species.

Negative Pleasura sees in the rising numbers of those least likely to progress along the path of human self-realization the preservation of its power. Negative Pleasura by its nature is emotional though its shrewdness is unquestioned. (One often encounters this surprising shrewdness in mentally disturbed individuals.) In questions of diminishment of its powers, it is nearsighted: for Negative Pleasura, the drive to power sidetracks it from the basic Pleasura requirement of survival (perhaps till too late). So that notwithstanding survival danger, the Negative Pleasura in certain cases has the "blinders," where overpopulation guarantees its continued power. One need only look at the obscene problem of world population today as an example.

One further point: one may ask how the Realitas arises from Pleasura if Negative Pleasura seems such a powerful influence? Is it Negative Pleasura that seeks to survive? The answer is that Pleasura, by the democratic rule of the preponderance of its elements so inclined, gravitates to the structuring of a Realitas. Negative Pleasura resentfully casts its vote with the majority if adequately convinced of the survival need, or is somehow "outvoted" by the balance of Pleasura, which is sufficiently alarmed about its survival.

A group in Negative Pleasura can, in the absence of conscience-restraint, inflict damage upon the external environment. That environment can also be the internal environment within a larger container, which it may share with other individuals or groups separate from and "alien" to itself who, by reason of that "alien-ness" become as much a target for the Negative Pleasura aggression as groups or things external to the overall group in which all the smaller groups in our example reside. The excesses of anti-Semitism in any society are always a relevant example, as is any type of bigotry.

Generally, these excesses cannot be blamed on the group as a whole but upon smaller subgroups of individuals or separate individuals themselves giving vent to the principle of brute force in contradistinction to surrendering this as part of the price of living within the community. Insofar as this principle is followed by these offending individuals they are —their patriotic and "conservative"-sounding protestations notwithstanding —potentially as lethal as revolutionaries who pose a danger to the peace and order of the state. They are barometers of a morbid set of prevailing circumstances (in terms of danger to the Realitas) as, for example, was the case in czarist Russia at the turn of the century. The pogroms that ravaged the country with unofficial czarist blessing and the widespread economic distresses made Bolshevik revolution predictable.

When there is a symbiotic coalition of Realitas and Pleasura a group becomes stable: the untrammeled claustrophobic energy of the group in Negative Pleasura becomes bottled up as a stopper is put on the pressure cooker by the Realitas. This "top" is administered in any number of ways. Apart from the obvious autocratic "terror" method of despots, the Realitas also utilizes community-sanctioned force (which Freud calls its "Right") to enforce the maintenance of the community rules concerning the social interactions of all the subject individuals. Further, the Realitas calls upon those positive parts of the group's Pleasura to aid it in its task: (a) the group's own Realitas desire to be governed; (b) the group's equivalent to Freudian super-ego phenomena (its conscience) ; (c) the group's own Pleasura drives for safety, security, and survival.

Lest there be confusion, although Realitas is considered the environment "external to the group," we are not here speaking of the "outside target" environment, as it were, which becomes the Pleasura group's subject matter for aggression: that is, Realitas as group environment is here strictly construed as the next outside environment, that which imposes order upon the turbulent group, bringing it to heel, bottling it and containing it. The environment which the group wreaks its havoc upon is that which is external to the group itself, the group at this time being comprised of both the controlling Realitas and the "controlled" group in Pleasura.

In short, "environment" to the Pleasura group is twofold:

(a) the controlling Realitas (the group's first order of environment, its "skin," as it were: see figure 1), and

(b) the outer (outside the whole group, Realitas and the "ruled" inclusive) "alien" environment, "target" groups, and things on the "outside" of the group's own environmental Realitas "skin" (see figure 2).

Figure 1

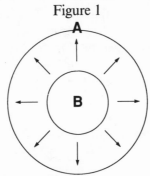

(A) The Realitas ruling environment
(B) The ruled group in Pleasura. (The arrows here and in figure 2 indicate the thrust of Negative-Pleasura force.)

Figure 2

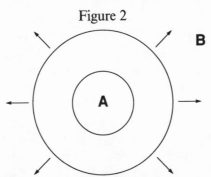

(A) The entire group entity, Realitas and Pleasura, as one group in Pleasura thrusting outwards, in its Negative-Pleasura force, against the external environment.
(B) The external, outside (of the group) environment.

Realitas is manifested in various forms of rule from the most rudimentary, to the most sophisticated, from the brute force of the most powerful warrior within a group of ruffians or outlaws or perhaps cave dwellers, through the spectrum cycle to the more sophisticated tyrant in charge of a governed state. Finally Realitas reaches through to the most positive end of the spectrum, namely, enlightened forms of self-government. Here we talk of that form of Realitas not forcefully imposed from without, but brought about at least in apparent pursuit of the elusive "will" of the majority of the people, as in democracies. Here, as we have observed before, the view can be put forward that this form of Realitas is a Pleasura choice: but in this case a predominantly positive one. The existence of democracies is evidence of the reason assessed "plateau of responsibility" of will. Assuming the group's Positive Pleasura to be in the ascendency, it seeks to impose and submit to a Realitas (such as "enlightened" self-government) that will assure the group being put on the pathway to human self-realization. Whether or not the group is ultimately able or wishes to proceed up that path, whether its Positive Pleasura will prevail in the face of its negative, is another story. But that is in the ultimate sense: in the immediate sense, Positive Pleasura, aided by reason, sees in democracy the realistic answers to both need (survival and necessity) and desire. There is a danger in the word "democracy" that is greatly overlooked. Like "freedom," positive connotations are so embedded in the word that Pleasura of the negative order is, as with the case of freedom, able to use it for its own purposes. The word "democracy" itself brings with it a set of blinkers which are affixed to the democratic onlooker, blinding him to Negative Pleasura excesses practiced in the so-called democracy. One need only look at some of the "generals"-type of autocratic systems of fear, euphemistically called democracies (in Central and South America). Under the banner of "democracy" Negative Pleasura can ride its wild tiger with much impunity and great leeway, knowing that the true democracies have sentimental sympathies for any sister system even merely calling itself democratic, so compelling are democracy's positive attributes. Democracy is as democracy does.

It may just be wishful thinking to postulate a psychological Positive Pleasura impulse of such a force and energy that it actually dictates a group's ultimate psychologically oriented choices. The acquisitive ends of Positive Pleasura are not, as we have discussed, of that degree of nostril-flaring vitality and dynamic allure as are the acquisitive ends of Pleasura seeking to satisfy the basic needs and desires.

In fairness, the Positive Pleasura goals can also be termed "needs" in that the resultant peace and harmony that they may bring ensures the basic survival of the species in general. But this thought is too vast and vague for many common minds to be able to get their Pleasura teeth into: those with potential to see and "feel" it as their own immediate and direct Pleasura needs are not members of the common herd, but belong to a small, natural group of intellectual thinkers and sincerely inspired ordinary individuals (as opposed to "poseurs," opportunists, and mere followers).

The specific type of Realitas manifested in the governing body is, to a large extent, dictated by the nature of the Pleasura it seeks to dominate: the more negative the state of Pleasura the group is in, the more negative and tyrannical the ruling Realitas. Likewise, the more positive the Pleasura of the group, the more enlightened the governing Realitas form. Minoan culture at its height was a harmonious mix of an unoppressive monarchy Realitas regime and an easy-going, tolerant, and open-spirited people. The art of the culture bespeaks this attitude in the people's manner and ways, in their light, tolerant good-humored attitude, in the relatively great freedom enjoyed by women. This was a peace-prone culture, bound soon to be overtaken, as we have seen earlier, by the Mycenean Greek "warrior" types. Thus, a civilized, relaxed, and peace-loving populace whose attitude was mirrored in that of the ruling Realitas. The difference is that between totalitarian regimes and those governments that are more democratic. One realizes that such examples are trite, but they work to make the point. There is no conscious aim to push democracy as the end of Positive Pleasura's highest goals; whatever the form of government or phase of civilization may be is hidden from our eyes (if such is ever achieved).

The grappling of Realitas and Pleasura within and through a group reflects the dynamics of nature as well. The ordering of the organic world is broken down into identifiable cells, tissues, and bodies—containers plus the contained. In the microcosmic realm of matter the interaction of elemental matter can from one point of view be considered individual, random, and free-ranging elemental particles (representing the Pleasura state) coming in contact with ordered, compliant structures of particles and being impressed into those structures and their orders (the Realitas state). These structures are added to and build greater levels of complexity until they surface from the infinite into the world of the finite and join the macrocosmic family of empirical phenomena, our sensible world.

The Realitas, then, is an ordering principle; the Pleasura Principle, in an ongoing dialectic confrontation with Realitas, is unrestrained and uninhibited. The Realitas is the restrictive principle of "Thou shalt not devour" or "Thou shalt devour only as I permit you to," whereas the principle of Pleasura is "I shall devour anything and everything as I alone will it."

In any group in a state of Negative Pleasura the ruler or ruling element must symbolically be identified with the Negative Pleasura of the group itself: that is, the group must see in the ruler a reflection of that Negative Pleasura which suffuses it, so that the ruler becomes a symbol of it. There is hardly an ethnic group or nation, no matter how insignificant, that does not have a "glory" period in its history, which upon close examination is generally a period of Negative Pleasura expansion and aggressions upon neighbors, centered upon some leader of the same blood as the people. The Mongol incursion westward into Europe during the thirteenth century, under Gengis Khan and his successors, in the main owed its very success to that same line of Mongol leaders. With the death of Ogdar Khan in 1242 and the uncertainty about the succession, the Mongol spirit of conquest started to wane. The vast empire began to split up. In 1294, with the death of Kublai Khan, the Mongol Pleasura phenomenon of remarkable conquest was over and the empire was disintegrating. After the death of Kublai Khan, there no longer was the esteemed titled position of "Grand Khan."

The survival of a nondemocratic Realitas relies upon certain necessary "tools" specially designed for that purpose. The Realitas needs more insurance for its perpetuation than mere symbols. In particular, with regard to groups in extreme Negative Pleasura: the Realitas ruling body must also be ready, willing, and able to control by another primitive and basic instinct as fundamental as the "blood," namely, fear or terror. So long as terror is reasonably imposed—so long as the group is reasonably in fear—notwithstanding any eventual group-grumbling or dissatisfaction, the Realitas will be soundly ensconced in its ruling position. Should that terror falter, the same group that once followed the Realitas leader with admiration and fidelity may rise up in its turn to terrorize or overthrow the leader or governing group. Again we have only to turn to the former Soviet Union as a recent example. On the other hand, China after Tiananmen Square shows the converse, i.e., how the maintance of terror prevails over an emerging Pleasura.

What of the hypothesis that the necessity of terror might be avoided by a gradual placating of the Pleasura group? The problem is that the original Negative Pleasura group brought the Realitas governing body to power and then was "contained by terror." But once that terror diminishes or becomes ineffective, a new Negative Pleasura rises up to incite rebellion against its leaders, given the right conditions.

If that Pleasura of the ruled is addressed forcefully (though not necessarily by force in the first instance), that is, if the "basic needs" causes of that Negative Pleasura, both real and imagined, are meaningfully and convincingly addressed (including convincing promises or lies), there could be a transitional period wherein the agitated, ruled group evolves from a state of "boiling over" to a more restrained and "containable" nature. In such a case, the Realitas leadership finds a degree of safety from the fury of the incensed group; indeed, if the transition period is managed successfully by the Realitas governor, the group may become reconciled to it again and permit it to continue in power for the time being. Such psychology was commonplace in the former Eastern bloc dictatorships with phrases such as "The Workers' Paradise" lulling (or attempting to lull) a deprived populace into the feeling of expectation that, if the "Paradise" is not here, it is coming soon.

Should the terror not be reinforced in the case of a Pleasura uprising, the Realitas governor may still manage to survive the storm in the event that the rebelling group lacks some of the fundamental prerequisites to actualize its Negative Pleasura. That is, in the case of a student revolt of the type in our earlier examples, such an uprising would be effective only if there is a keen and strong unifying identification akin to "blood-ness." That of course becomes a problem in the diversity of student groups. Further, the groups themselves, being of an intellectual stamp so far as the masses are concerned, lack the power of being the symbol for the greater masses in terms of a wide and universal emotional identification. (Student protests during the Vietnam war were not immediately embraced by the broader public.) Eric Hoffer, quoting from Lincoln Steffens,* noted that the intellectual would rather work, fight, or talk for liberty than have it. This cynical observation does impart the truth of the restless, upsurging Pleasura energy in the intellectuals as contrasted to the quiet acceptance and desire to be left alone in the hearts of a needs-serviced populace.

By contrast, in the Russian and French revolutions not only students but sailors, workers, and the masses arose, all linked by a common bond—they were not aristocrats. All the various segments of the group found a unity in being the oppressed of the aristocracy, they were the "tormented," not the tormentors. In the Russian revolution of course there was the added unifying factor of "not being capitalist."

Negative Pleasura manifested in an emerging revolutionary group must still in order to succeed in its aims place its reliance not only upon the expounding of social ideals but must invoke the more basic and elemental Pleasura-bonding factors.

The term "proletariat" was particularly appealing for Negative Pleasura in the Russian Revolution. Its Marxist image was inseparable from the Pleasura-rousing word "oppressed." Action words and jargon denoting extravagant oppression found their way easily into the revolution, as they always do: "the workers and "the proletariat" are "crushed," "trammeled," "squeezed dry," "eviscerated," "ground down," "crushed under the

---

The Autobiography of Lincoln Steffens, New York: Harcourt Brace, 1931. Eric Hoffer, *The Ordeal of Change,* New York: Harper & Row, 1963, p. 100.

heel of" all images denoting a helpless insect having its insides squashed out by the ruthless grinding from above. There is a vital and early precedent in Western civilization for this type of terminology. In the Old Testament the prophet Amos cries from the heart to the rich that they not grind the face of the poor in the dust. His was a conscious invocation, an early clarion call for humane treatment of the poor and the needy.

Transferring the "squeezed dry" and "eviscerated" metaphor to the immediate human image, blood and bloodiness are evoked: The magic "blood," the heady "blood," the intoxicating "blood"!

And so as the artificial designation of proletariat becomes swathed in the image of blood (the blood of the workers) it becomes precious and to be preserved and propagated. Their unifying flag becomes the color of blood; at last, the openly and immediately understood blood identification like a religious icon. Their army becomes the "red" army, and as the magic of their "blood" ensures victories for the upward thrusting pleasura, their star is rising, a red star. But they are not the first to use the "blood" flag for its potency of appeal: the English royalty have long utilized the blood-red banner background. Charles I was able to summon royal supporters to his red banner, in effect saying "Protect the royal blood," indeed, "Join with the royal blood against Cromwell."

In terms of the Russian Revolution, there was an important address-ing of the elemental Pleasura factor of self-esteem with the positive iden-tification of being "something" as opposed to being "not-something," that is, being a worker, being the "employed" as opposed to the "employer." In the new regime being propelled by the Pleasura the proletariat was imaged as worthy, whereas the bourgeoisie/capitalists had no worth: the latter in Marxist perspective are "enemies" of the people, and if they have worth, it is only as targets for bullets.

Further, as we saw above, to stimulate and encourage the emotionalism of the "blood," the Negative Pleasura group will try to appeal to the most primitive roots by drawing upon the basic "blood" relationship words: the family will be invoked. Thus, socialist and trade union movements refer to their memberships as "brotherhoods," thereby drawing from secret societies as old as antiquity who survived intact by artificially stimulating an aura of close blood-relationship that would appeal, the "brethren" appeal: "help me brother." Groups manifesting Negative Pleasura in terms of "territory" and nationalism seek to get the brethren to rally round the cause of the blood parent, the "Motherland," the "Fatherland."

Except for the recent racial identification strategies of blacks in the United States who refer to themselves in the "brother" and "sister" mode, one seems to find that where a group already is of a blood relationship, e.g., where a group is primarily the same blood racial type it does not have to perpetually use the brother-and-sister label. Rather, it is so universally implied and understood, with such apparent ease and confidence, that more casual social terms come to be utilized. In some cases, Pleasura may be stimulated and kept at a boil by passing up the elementary and rousing blood terms for the informal brotherly-type friendship appellations. The strength of this tactic implies that the confidence in the blood relationship is so self-evident that invoking it becomes redundant and the more casual terminology may assuredly be used.

There is also a practical benefit to be gained here (and the Pleasura, in spite of its organic inclinations, is nothing if not practical in achieving its aims): that is, the nonblood terminology opens a wider scope of embracing those individuals who are other than of-the-blood, people who always find themselves swept up in the Pleasura current of another biological group. So one finds that where there is the same basic biological stock, as with the Russians or the Germans in their wars of Negative Pleasura, the obvious blood relationship does not have to be brought forth: rather, the more offhanded "comrade" is used in that the blood relationship is so far and away acknowledged as a fundamental binding basis that it needn't be referred to and that indeed a social rather than a biological bond can be addressed, namely, comradeship.

Even if the Realitas group is not strong and its terror is not feared or respected to a degree more than the sense of injustice and indignation experienced by the group, nevertheless if (1) there is a strong present recollection of successful terror, and (2) if there is no blatant unifying bond e.g., "blood," "patriotism," or the like, then the group and its revolt will fail. Even the recollection of former feared terror and imposition of strong authoritarian order may well prove sufficient to bring the "revolting" group "back to its senses," as the Realitas group might put it, in the absence of the necessary quality of unifying bond. The recent uprising of Chinese students in Beijing fired the imagination and the indignation of similar student groups in other major cities of China. The uprising spread and was joined by politicians, teachers and professors, and even ordinary members of the public. Testing the Realitas waters, these people came to sense a time of vulnerability of the Realitas rulers, especially in light of a perceived initial reluctance on the part of these rulers to use terror. However, apart from the very loose-fitting cloak of studentship and the very wide-ranging and (in terms of Negative Pleasura) somewhat intangible grievances of corruption, etc., the group of rebelling students could not invoke a universal mass identification in terms of being victims of some Pleasura-rousing grievance or "injustice." In effect, substantial elements of Negative Pleasura invocation were lacking. That is, there was no one common "blood"-type equivalent identification of a universally accepted nature (within China) that the oppressed could focus on. There was no "proletariat," "worker," or other unifying term to highlight and rally people. The only identification to unify the group was that of "nonpolitician" versus "politicians," and that standing by itself is too vague. The Pleasura needs "red meat" to sink its teeth into for its Jekyll-and-Hyde transformation to the negative state to occur. Otherwise, the emerging Pleasura is little more than indignation. Returning as well to the picture of the farflung Roman Empire without broad means of communication in the time of the later barbarian invasions, so too, is the case with the vast numbers of remote Chinese peasants of today. Their means of and access to communication, especially with the world and realities outside China, are far more limited than that of the intellectuals and more privileged masses in the major cities. Good communication of vital grievances, and of propaganda in that regard, is a necessary binding factor of revolution, leading as it does to necessary mass participation in the general Negative Pleasura. The Negative Pleasura of those who seek to overthrow must be shared by those they seek to lead.

Also, "injustice" founded only on general principles instead of hardcore specific realities (it is best for the Negative Pleasura proponent if even one lone specific bone of contention can be found) cannot actualize the potential for Negative Pleasura; at best it can only do so with great difficulty, in the absence of widespread support within the group.

Shrewd revolutionaries inherently understand the weaker aspects of human nature and have always laid great stress upon the tool of propaganda. Their philosophy is that if the lie is great enough and adequately geared to incite Negative Pleasura, it will be "believed" sufficiently to arouse the mass reaction desired. In *Mein Kampf* Hitler berated the Kaiser's regime for its inadequate propaganda, referring to it as ambiguous, ineffectual, and ultimately "useless." In that work Hitler became a type of latter-day advocate for propaganda, even setting out the rules, namely, that it must utilize only a few points, that these points must be the "simplest ideas" and must be repeated thousands of times, that the slogan must be the end in itself, and so on. He declared that propaganda's results will amaze "beyond understanding." The truth of these advertisements for propaganda was shown only too effectively by the enormity of Josef Goebbels's success in influencing so many German people and their numerous international sympathizers at the time.

In considering the recent failed Chinese example aren't we really addressing the simple question of whether or not the "group" is in a state of Negative Pleasura? If not, for reasons ranging from lack of widespread communication to fear due to recently remembered terror, to far-ranging and perhaps antithetic diversities, the overall bottom-line impulse quality of the group may not be one of Negative Pleasura, in spite of the fact that a small proportion of it—the "firebrands"—are substantially in such a state. In the Chinese attempt, the universality of arousal was missing.

In the French Revolution the country, insofar as the large masses of the population were concerned, was in a bankrupt state, (in part due to the war in America) and the people were suffering from lack of need-satisfaction. The conditions of general deprivation were accelerated and exacerbated by the fall of Marie Antoinette's favorite minister of finance, Calonne, a man who manufactured money as if out of the air, rolling over royal loans and national debts into a towering pyramid of worthless paper. The stupidity of the landed gentry also fueled the general "righteous ire" of the mass Pleasura in that, in spite of the reality of the enormous mass need and volcanic discontent, they refused Calonne's proposal to aid the situation by subsidies to be levied on real-estate holdings. This was a clear adversarial statement of not "caring," a perceived desire to continue to crush the faces of the masses in the dust. It could therefore be said that, quantitatively, the "group" (the masses) here was in a state of potential and actual Negative Pleasura, and the group could therefore be universally ignited by the "firebrands" (the Robespierres). It is a strange phenomenon that often one may perceive an almost suicidal determination of the besieged Realitas to continue its provocative activities or attitudes toward an arising populace in Pleasura, as if intent on egging them on further to the Realitas's ultimate destruction. If examples are needed, I refer the reader to Charles I in the time of Cromwell and also to the French royalty and nobility prior to the revolution. Does this sort of reaction reflect a natural death wish of the Realitas, a Freudian wish to self-destruction? Is this a phase of the dialectic of impulse? At a certain point in the dialectic, does a Realitas desire to be crushed arise, much as the populace, at a certain juncture, desires to be strongly ruled? Does the Pleasura, seeing a new foothold of power, inflate the personal Negative Pleasuras of the Realitas's leaders and establishment, such as stiff-necked pride and refusal to grant concessions in the face of approaching disaster? Or, if, as we have queried above, it is a death wish of the Realitas, is such a drive simply a part of the Negative Pleasura of the Realitas itself? The answer is probably a combination of the latter and the phasing process of the dialectic itself.

A digression here is in order. Any Pleasura impulse to self-destruction must be looked upon as abnormal, as an anomaly in that it runs counter to the main nature and essence of Pleasura itself, namely, self-survival and perpetuation.

In China's Tiananmen Square uprising, one of the potentials for

Negative Pleasura was indeed present: all of the members of the uprising group (the "firebrands") were of the same blood and racial type—they were all Chinese. But it is not enough for group members to be "of the blood" with nothing else to inspire action. The "blood" factor standing by itself has no fire lit under it: coupled with "the blood" there must be universal resentment or negative emotional reaction of some kind on a mass scale threatening to vindicate the blood. Here, apart from the real resentment of the relatively small student and intellectual segment of the population, in the main this strong emotion was not universally shared by the majority.

Studentship itself is a temporal thing; it is a period lasting only a few years, and then the individual who bears that identity changes into a graduate, then into a professional or a career person, etc. So that the "student" relationship is in itself not so strong and binding, in the order of the more permanent Pleasura categories, e.g., religious membership, to call forth Negative Pleasura as a result of injustice. When he was a student, the late Abby Hoffmann said that anybody over thirty should not be trusted: that is, in effect, anyone who is older than a student should not be trusted. In later life he declared that anyone *under* thirty should be not trusted. Social strata that are of such a temporal nature find difficulty in being the stuff of which Negative Pleasura is made.

A student revolt is only of serious consequence to the ruling Realitas if the masses are universally behind it, identifying Pleasura with its goals and seeing in the students a needed symbol, an igniting spark. Such was the case in the Hungarian revolution of 1956. As the rebellious students marched down the streets of Budapest, men standing on the sidewalks doffed their hats and women cheered. If the masses are apathetic or fearful (among other things) the threat to the Realitas is only minimal and temporary. The Hungarian revolution's failure at this point is an illustration of the then will of the Soviet Realitas leaders to impose terror in strength. They sent the tanks and soldiers in with instructions to shoot. The population was unarmed, and though it had the Pleasura will to rise up, the will and means of the Soviet terror by far exceeded the material significance of the Pleasura of Hungary's masses.

When the steam finally ran out of those in Tiananmen Square the great numbers of the collected student groups simply got up and began to walk home. The Realitas group, the Chinese rulers, though the terror they had previously invoked was not adequately feared by the students (or the uprising would not have materialized in such a public and defiant way) simply had to wait the storm out. At first, they did not even know that this is what they were doing, for they were mostly thunderstruck themselves at the occurrence of this "revolt" and reacted at first by uncharacteristic gestures of understanding and even hinted at compromise.

But the rebellious group, not being able to spark a mass uprising (the mass elements being lacking as well as the absence of one or more strong leaders) simply fell apart in the face of the continuing Realitas and in the face, no doubt, of recent recollections of its former terror and hard authoritarian domination (which the governing Realitas was quick to assert after it had regained its composure).

The abortive Chinese uprising drew its astonishing though short-lived strength primarily from an essentially positive Pleasura theme, namely, a cry for democracy: this was the rallying banner in priority to demands for reforms and cries against corruption in high places. But the masses of Chinese are not sufficiently knowledgeable about the advantages of democracy for purposes of self-realization, nor of the practical "spin-off" economic advantages. Furthermore, Chinese culture is perhaps a more alien creature to the principles of democracy than is that of the West. In the West, the stress is upon individual "rights" and his or her Pleasura, whereas in Chinese culture the individual Pleasura is outweighed by the individual "desire-to-be ruled" Realitas impulse.

Further, Chinese culture stresses the overweighing importance of the group as opposed to that of the "individual," the darling of democracy. In such circumstances the lack of widespread mass democratic sympathy and Pleasura-igniting potential is understandable. What little attraction democracy would presently seem to hold for them is perhaps outweighed by their fear of and respect for the Realitas terror of old.

Democracy, when it works, aims at the "harmony" of Realitas and Pleasura insofar as any accord can be achieved or pretended at between the two. In order to assure its perpetuation the Realitas, as manifested in a democratic society, declines to permanently identify itself with any one part of the group: democratic Realitas tolerates and thereby acknowledges, in its shrewdness and perhaps its wisdom (a word with connotations that must be weighed carefully in each case), the variability of the vessels of social-psychological impulse manifestation: in this case, the variability of those who will govern. Thus, in a democracy no one part of the group is excluded from aspiring to the important order, for what is more intrinsic and desirable than power to the Pleasura in the hearts of man, especially the power of ruling?

This is not to imply that in a democracy there is some permanent and very shrewd subterranean group that perpetuates itself as the true "Richelieu" Realitas through a progression of Realitas-variables. Rather, to understand the nature of these two impulses and their operation, one is aided by personifying them in order that we may draw a step further away from the abstract.

Let us therfore view the democratic Realitas as a determined ruler, whether directly or indirectly, who shrewdly manipulates his mode and agents of rule with a view to perpetuating his own control and domination. This determined ruler is practical to the extreme, patient, and opportunistic. Understanding the nature of a democracy as "majority" rule, and understanding as well that the choices of the majority are variables (except for the invariable antidespot sentiment of the majority), it therefore encourages the illusion of variability while in reality giving the majority a continuing offering of limited choices, these being tried-and-true agencies of its power. Thus, in most democracies there are generally a limited number of political parties vying for power—in the United States there are two; in England, three (including the Liberals), etc. Even in other Western countries where more parties may abound, the same two or three usually dominate. This method of governing enables a continuation of Realitas-ruling power as opposed to its antithesis, anarchy (or on a lesser scale, an instability of government, e.g., the rapid series of governments as in Germany in the 1920s, France in the 1950s, and in post–World War II Italy).

An unstable Realitas results in confusion and insecurity in the group ruled. In the politically uncertain and unstable climate of pre-imperial Rome, there was a feeling in the people that they were ready to be led, to be given order and direction. The pathway to the imperial autocracies of the Caesars was thus paved. Also, if we return to the example of Ancient Egypt, we find that at the end of the pyramid age and the reign of absolute monarchs, a long stretch of disorder and anarchy set in. The throne of Egypt was occupied by a succession of weak kings, lacking strength to control and maintain their rule and Realitas: for example, seventy separate kings ruled for seventy days in the seventh dynasty. The result was lawlessness, a descent into further disorder, and a splitting up of the country again into a number of smaller states. Being ready for strong rule now, the land fell into a feudalism of ascending orders of strength, in classical feudal fashion, from lords up to the kings. The country was ready and accepting of some form of strong ruler.

From December 1916 on Russia after the assassination of Rasputin witnessed all sorts of remedial governing and political actions. By March of 1917 things were in a chaotic state: there were food riots, arrests, attempted repression of the Duma (the Russian assembly), and finally on March 15 an attempt made at provisional government under Prince Lvoff coupled with the czar's abdication. There was talk and hope of reason, new moderate leaders, even restoration of the czar. But the people were fed up. The indecisiveness and disorder swayed them to the side of a strong desire to be ruled by a new order, one that promised relief from all this chaos. All this paved the way to the final seizing of power by the Bolsheviks on November 7, 1917.

The social-psychological method of historical observation is susceptible to internal conflict. For example, we have earlier said that what we arbitrarily deem to be Negative Pleasura by virtue of the criterion of force may, in terms of human values, be deemed "good" as in the case of rebellions that overthrow dictators. Likewise, on the other side of the Realitas coin, the desire to be ruled may, in Freudian terms, be viewed as a step in the right direction in terms of the process of civilization. Depending upon the circumstances, this impulse to be ruled can at the same time be a step backward into the arms of autocracy and dictatorship.

The goal of Realitas in democracy is psychologically aided and abetted by the device of universal suffrage. Allowing each group member a vote (and therefore some political influence or power) appeals to the Pleasura phenomenon of "Will to Power" in both the individual and the governed group, those who are commanded as a whole. Thus, the Realitas phenomenon (as a political system) in a democratic society is further assured of its perpetuation by appealing to basic Pleasura: "You the individuals rule, you the group rule. Therefore you rule yourselves. Therefore, you do not need to feel claustrophobic: you are not being 'contained' by external forces. You are, rather, governing yourself, or, in short, doing as you will." Even totalitarian regimes understand this mass appeal, and so often they insert the word "peoples" or "democratic" as adjectives describing their society and political systems. In democracies it just so happens that, within the limitations that may prevail in the given political system, the people come as close to ruling as can ever be reasonably expected to happen. As a result, a democracy is generally the safest sort of governing system for the Realitas and its objectives of stability and permanence insofar as pent-up claustrophobic energy is indeed substantially lacking. Democracy in the main is a healthy creature with a certain immunity to disruptive Negative Pleasura. Yet this can change on the turn of a dime, as witnessed in the democratic government of Germany of 1933 as it moved toward Hitler's dictatorship.

Having said that, let us also examine the warts of a democratic Realitas system. As we have earlier suggested, in fact, the real and practical power in democracies is in the hands of the few who control the political system of the society, the party politicians. To this extent one sees a partial throwback to the political cynicism and gerrymandering of the politicians of Rome in the unstable aftermath of the defeat of Carthage. It is these few men who narrow down the objects of popular suffrage to the very limited choices of which we have spoken: this has to be for the expediency of ruling, otherwise the Realitas becomes too divided against itself and cannot survive because its formulation is too impractical to rule. But in its necessary limited selectness, this system of suffrage-control beckons to Negative Pleasura as "opportunity knocking."

Universal suffrage is fine and good, but in practice democracy is only two or three choices away from totalitarianism. That is, in most totalitarian societies, so-called democratic elections give the voters usually one choice only, namely, the ruling and generally the only party. In a democracy there is generally one choice more—the opposition party (and sometimes third or fourth choices in terms of smaller, weaker political entities). In practice only one extra choice often differentiates a democracy from a totalitarian regime, in terms of the exercise of the vote by the masses. Next enters the "majority-as-all" fiction: since the majority will have voted in the government, it certainly was not a unanimous choice. But here a fiction enters perpetuated by the Realitas to placate the group Pleasura: majority rule becomes equated with "all the individuals," so that the nation sees its government described and embodied in phrases like, "government by the people" wherein it is somehow substantially all the people who govern, through their elected leaders.

Let it not be misunderstood that we are glibly differentiating a democracy from a totalitarian regime simply by virtue of one extra voting choice: that is only one—though a significant—differentiation. Others abound, the most important being that despots, no matter how placid they are on the surface, must continually batten down the hatches of pent-up claustrophobic energy: this is not the case in democracies (though they have other ailments peculiar to "free" societies). Therefore despots, as compared to democracies, are of necessity in a constant state of instability, notwithstanding appearances to the contrary.

Thus, practically speaking, contemporary democracy is not, in terms of its Realitas, the rule of all of the people. Rather, it is often rule by one of very narrowed-down political interests. In ancient Greece democracy at first was oligarchic (rule by the few) in that the aristocrats ruled the many. Eventually Greek democracy, by extension of the vote to all the citizens, became rule by the many—"citizens," that is. Slaves, non-Athenians and noncitizens representing great numbers of individuals circumnavigating within Athens, lacked the franchise. Thus it can be said that again the Realitas of Athens was an oligarchic form of democracy in that it was rule of the many by the "few" again, this time the "few" being the citizens. Oddly enough, the Athenian Pleasura of the citizenry gives rise to early hints of socialism, with special grants and fees being accorded to all citizens and taxation being imposed on all including the aristocracy.

In modern American democracy the argument can be made that the American Realitas is oligarchic in nature in that the "few," namely, two political parties rule the many.

The Realitas is ingenious here in mesmerizing the group into believing that either one or the other of the two major "adversary" political groups actually represents a substantially large percentage of individuals forming the group and their interests. It is a polished marketing job but in practical terms one that is beneficial to stability and all of the potentially positive results that are the legacy of a stable and free society, and does not turn out to be inimical to the traditions of freedom. As well democracy is probably the best working example of politics in action, with the United States and its great diverse interaction of different vying political interests as the most dynamic illustration. A system providing for input from all sorts of included diverse interests is one that constructively gives outlet to the varied Pleasuras of inclusive subgroups within the country. "Politics is, as it were, an interaction between the mutual dependence of the whole and some sense of independence of the parts."* Let us then treat the system as that of majority consensus and indeed "rule" (with the caveat of the "opportunity-knocking" therein for Negative Pleasura, complacency being the most immediate door-opener to these opportunities).

Having thus looked at the bloom on the rose let us now observe the thorns. In the end majority rule may be self-defeating in that the majority may always, by the law of averages, be mediocre in ability and intelligence. Eventually, this must come to be more and more represented in the interim ruling classes, and to that extent, their power to perpetuate their own mediocrity of interests and aspirations will effectively make itself felt. In fact in such a case, the mediocre may inherit the earth. But if "survival of the fittest" is a meaningful slogan, the truth may be that the mediocre, though unglamorous and unheroic, are in fact the fittest. Let it be explained that "mediocre" here is not only referring merely to those with lack of Pleasura-type self-assertiveness but also to those who are, at best, only average in terms of intellect, talent, and capability. There is a paradox concerning all of the foregoing criticisms of systems multiplying the lowest common denominator of man. To an extent the large majority of ungifted and average persons must necessarily exist as a mass pool within which the few frogs of excellence can croak away and jump upon the lily pads. A utopian society of equals of intellect and ability would not be a desirable situation for some who would thereby lose their special status. At our present stage of human intellectual development, Pleasura still propels some

---

*Crick, *In Defence of Politics*, p. 140.

intellectual powerhouse leaders, shakers and movers by the tail-feathers of their vanity, and by their own perceptions that they are head and shoulders above the mass of the great unwashed. Being equals among equals would be no good for the mass of these "special" people; their motivation to do what they do best from which humanity so often greatly benefits would be removed, for who would be their mass spectators, admirers, and applauders?

The political danger of mediocrity is its ability to be manipulated, and its readiness to be complacent if presented with satisfaction of basic needs. Also the "mediocre" is not that type of vehicle in which Positive Pleasura can race on toward "end good" goals. Who is to say whether mediocrity is a genetic state on a large scale, or whether it is a phenomenon of potentiality unrealized? That is, were higher and liberal education more widespread and tailored to the lesser abilities of many, would not thereby avenues of objectivity and of curiosity leading to inquiry thus open perhaps to many who are resigned, from early childhood, to a life of beer and "couch potatoness"? Negative Pleasura, however, seeks a mass foundation of unthinking "couch potatoness" as an assurance of a certain brake against human progression toward self-realization: in proportion to which humanity progresses toward that goal, the ascendency of Positive Pleasura in company with reason presents a rising threat to Negative Pleasura of diminishment of and control over its not-inconsiderable powers.

8

Leadership

The potential of Pleasura to manifest itself in both its positive and negative forms must of necessity have the prevailing factor of relevant leadership. Pleasura is a highly subjective phenomenon; it manifests itself in the collective group mind like a highly exciting stimulant, or perhaps it is more apt to say intoxicant. But a leaderless group, regardless of its state of excitement, is impotent to act in any significant way. It is too disjointed. Its efforts will be dissipated in many directions. The erupting claustrophobic energy must be controlled, harnessed, channeled, and directed: that is the role of leadership.

Leadership can take the form of a single person, a group, or a committee. The leader or the group must be a reflection of the entire group's subjective consciousness. That is, the group must be able to identify dynamically and emotionally with an individual leader or the committee of leadership: that identification must be such to which the members of the group can project themselves as well as their hopes, fears, and ambitions: in short, their total subjective Pleasura state must be able to be projected onto the single or collective leader, who, in a sense, becomes their alter ego. This was certainly Lenin's desire for the mass perception as it related to the "soviets," the Bolshevik "councils." These "soviets" supposedly represented workers and ordinary soldiers.

It is difficult to inventory the requirements that go into the composition of such a leader or a group of leaders. As we have noted, there must be some one quality or set of qualities that leads to the identification and factors just spoken of. One factor seems to stand clear with the bulk of leaders in Negative Pleasura situations: to a greater or lesser extent, they have charisma. The most extraordinary example in recent times is that of Hitler.

Some studies seem to indicate that charisma is in fact a physio-chemical phenomenon, that some element is transmitted from the charismatic leader to the immediate followers, thereby infusing them with the leader's energy, fortified by their devotion. The spectacle of this energy and devotion in the leadership group has the desired effects upon the group itself. Charisma may well be artificially developed in part by theatrics: Hitler took coaching in oration and spent much time in front of mirrors practicing his oratorical "dramatic" poses. But whatever the answer to the riddle of charisma may be, whether chemical or psychological, without that element the substantial potential of Negative Pleasura within a group has difficulty in being realized.

Charisma is an especially important quality for the leader or leadership group: if the dynamics of the Negative Pleasura group phenomenon are effected successfully, then the group will come to have dominion over part of its environment, including groups that may be part of that dominion. The leader becomes the focal point for the Negative Pleasura drive outward onto the external environment: he, she, or they become the personification of that drive, the tip of the spear. The leader becomes a symbol of that drive, and a symbol for all of the Pleasura urgings and passions in the group drive for self-gratification. More than this, as the group projects this drive and all of the mass Negative Pleasura aspirations onto the person and symbolism of the leader, he comes to stand for more: he represents not only the desire for self-gratification, but also the "want" cry, as it were, invoking the need requirements of the group. In other words, he also becomes the group's symbolic answer to the requirements of necessity: in a sense, he therefore becomes an image dear to survival Pleasura, a parent figure, a father figure, an older brother figure, the supplier of necessities, and if not immediately satisfying these needs, he embodies the hope for their future fulfillment. In this role he is augmenting the concepts of "blood," "family," and nation, personifications in himself that we discussed earlier.

A strange combination of symbolism comes to be equated with the head of a totalitarian state: at one and the same time he embodies terror yet serves the nation's parental role, the benevolent father. Combined simultaneously in one leader are the parent-image component to keep the measure of the Pleasura forces at bay so that they will not overflow, but remain contained within the parameters of domination by the leader, and all of the unbounded aspirations of Negative Pleasura as well as the expectations for satisfaction of need requirements. The industrialists of imperial Germany at the beginning of the twentieth century found much to praise in the strutting antics of the Kaiser, as would their successors thirty years later in Hitler. The Kaiser in proclaiming the need for Germany, like imperial Rome, to expand and impose itself, and in invoking *Weltmacht* and supporting it with the creation of a large fleet of battleships, had the ear of the industrialists as did Hitler when he orated of the need for German *Lebensraum*. When the Kaiser warmly intoned that Germany was in her shining armor, the princes of German industry, in their own flush of power-and-profit Pleasura, supported his public image and promoted the enhancement of the aura of national (and Negative) Pleasura, enfolding him: "Hoch der Kaiser!" later to become "Heil Hitler!"

The successful leader who maintains and plays with the Pleasura of the governed group, who dominates and controls it, and who maintains his dominion, is the leader who know how to control the necessary balance, that is, maintaining the order of Realitas, and invoking his Pleasura personification appeal. If he can successfully maintain the benign "father" type of imagery he will certainly have achieved a coup, for if Freud is right there is no childhood need as strong as the need for a father's protection. It is not only despotic rulers who can successfully employ such an image: in America's democracy witness the power of a Theodore or Franklin Roosevelt whose great appeal to the suffering and needy American masses was in great part as a father image.

We have spoken of the success of Napoleon Bonaparte in utilizing the revolutionary Pleasura of the French masses to embody, in his person, the counterpart of that Pleasura. With that power, had he, like Cromwell, subordinated his own Pleasura to the ideals that stimulated and propelled the French Revolution, no doubt all of Europe would have fallen under his sway. If ever there was an opportunity for a United States of Europe to arise in a paroxysm of idealism surmounting ethnicity it was then, especially since the nationalism of a united Germany had not yet arisen. (It was he in fact who would combine all the German principalities into a united and national unity, for efficiency of adminstration.) The attractive goal of "equality" for the European masses could have been so magnetic in its power to culminate the latent and ongoing mass-Pleasura that had arisen with the peasant revolts of the eleventh century and of which we have spoken. This culmination could have manifested itself into some great democratic United States of Europe that might have harnessed the Pleasura energies of nineteenth- and twentieth-century Europe into more positive paths than those finally taken. So much gain or loss for humanity—so much revolves about the person of one man, from time to time: so great, so vital is the Pleasura power of the leader, the one over the many millions, the one individual Pleasura over the destinies and fate of masses comprising the many millions, an incredible irony of which Negative Pleasura is well aware. Only rarely in human history is power given to an emerging Positive Pleasura on an international scale, to be able to do the near impossible, to capture the Pleasura of the masses with equal intensity to that of Negative Pleasura. But Negative Pleasura is ever watch-ful, and at the last moment it throws a monkey wrench into the works. Thus ancient Roman republicanism and embodiment, on a world scale, of justice and rule of law failed by the first century, brought down by the development and corruption of money, greed, self-gratification, base-ness and immorality of politicians and mean-spiritedness of the few very wealthy. And so it was with Napoleonic France, the carrier of the new Positive Pleasura flames of liberty and the great positive ideas. But Nega-tive Pleasura, seeming to delight as it always does in tantalizing human-ity with dreams of immanent ascendency to the higher Positive Pleasura plateaus, again threw in its secret weapon, ironically and tragically, the man who had symbolized it all, Napoleon. Negative Pleasura clothed him in its own mantle of self-indulgence and all the vulgarities of pride and petty social-climbing. At one blow the brightest chance for a United States of Europe went out like a dowsed light, and in the returning darkness ethnicity reestablished its old lines and bayed to the moon again with its old, blood-hunger howls. Today, the howling fills the lands of Serbs and Croats and Negative Pleasura rides the wild tiger through bloodied streets. Perhaps another charismatic leader is necessary for the weak race of humans to be brought together in unification for the positive rather than disintegration and polarization. Perhaps a Napoleon could have given France a greater-than-slim 51 percent vote for the European unity of Maastricht.

In the face of all the potential for the positive, Bonaparte becomes an example of the "fraility of the flesh" prostrating himself to personal Pleasura and bypassing idealistic opportunity. As one writer has put it, he would rather become the son-in-law of the old world than the incan-descent leader of the new. He crowned himself emperor and married a Hapsburg princess with a view to instituting his own old-world-type dynasty. Beethoven, indicative of the esteem in which the (till then) romantic hero was held by the romantic idealists and intellectuals of Europe, scratched out his name on the dedication Frontispiece to the symphony he had written in Napoleon's honor, renaming it instead the *Eroica*. The act was symbolic of a universal European disillusionment with the man and the subsequent crumbling of the foundations of the Realitas he had estab-lished, which in turn might have been itself the foundation for a Realitas of a greater Europe united under France and its revolutionary ideals.

Hoffer has said that absolute power is the manifestation most inimical to human uniqueness in that it always seeks to turn man into a thing and regress him back from his more advanced state to the matrix of nature.*

---

*Hoffer, p. 120.

Hoffer does not go on further as he might however, to inform that the leader who has absolute power seeks, albeit unconsciously (and generally successfully), to turn himself into a thing also. He does this with the help of Negative Pleasura, which raises the heady cup of power to his dribbling lips again, and again, and still again until objectivity is totally obscured by megalomania. In this state, he is the willing tool of Negative Pleasura and the wild ride on the tiger begins again. Bernard Crick* sees the leader as a victim of the leadership situation as well, but by an interesting process of deflection. He says that implicit in the act of leading is the treating of the ruled as things: the necessity for the leader so to do, in turn demoralizes him.

The ultimate demoralization of a leader is the fascist state, although whether he is demoralized (or immoral) before taking control becomes a chicken-and-egg question. Fascism is the form of government most suited to Negative Pleasura in its most extreme forms. For, wanting "things" to control instead of people, its accessory becomes the fascist state whose policy, as a Realitas, is to turn people into things in order to perpetuate its absolute power. "Things" are more efficient to govern and control than people. And as the taste of control that comes with fascist power is cultivated, it grows, fanned by the bellows of insatiable Negative Pleasura. It is helped by the other side of the Realitas coin—the desire to be governed, but the part of that side of the coin minted by Negative Pleasura, namely, the desire to be reduced down to a thing, the desire to lose one's humanness and be governed like one of many things stacked in a box. This is Negative Pleasura's deal with him who volunteers to be a fascist subject: "in return for your becoming a thing, I will free you of the burden of conscience." This freedom allows the fascist subject to strut, bully, torture, rape, and kill with impunity from remorse, for his victim has become a thing. The fascist Realitas government meantime, having only things to control, easily takes control of everything—political, cultural, industrial, religious, social. Ameba-like, it envelops and consumes all things, while Negative Pleasura applauds. It removes the basic liberties and freedoms of its subjects (whom it praises as superior to all other things and people), freedom of travel and so on, for things, unlike people, do not require freedoms. It promises its things a replacement for the humanity it has taken away from them, namely, national (and/or racial) glory. To this end, much to the satisfaction of Negative Pleasura, it arms for war, for a fascist state deems that without war there can be no glory. The reason for this is that such a state, not under the influence of Positive Pleasura, sees no good in positive ends such as advancement in research beneficial

---

*Professor of Politics and author of *The American Science of Politics*.

to humanity, promotion of the arts, and so on. Rather, its interests are nailed into the extreme and most shadowy end of Negative Pleasura, the bloody part of the spectrum. That is where it must find its glory and that is why Negative Pleasura has provided it with such absolute power. This is the ride on the tiger with its claws unsheathed. And because things do not oppose—only humans oppose—the state removes all opposition of any nature whether in newspapers, legislatures, or wherever. The state stacks all these places, universities, courts, etc., with its things, stacked in rows like identically stamped bottles. Then the self-gratification of cruelty and depravity can begin unhindered. Because things have no freedoms, they must be secretly watched lest they behave like humans, and so a strong and brutal secret police is set in place to watch the many stacked rows of things and ensure that none of them become restless and begins to behave like humans, wishing to get out of their places, or complain, and so on. Beginning with this empowered secret police, sadistic self-gratification is given full license, for the subject matter of that gratification is things. Then onward and upward, through the ordinary police, the military, and the ordinary people, now things mesmerized into believing that they are "thing-gods." Therefore all inferior beings (so designated by the state) are fair game for gratification of all brutish desires and impulses. This, then, is fascism, the utopia of things.

9

Tribes, Blood within Blood, and Territory

Having set out on a straightforward path to the phenomenon of Negative Pleasura via the major signposts of "blood" and "territory," we now, to our dismay, are informed by travelers about still farther signposts on yet other roads, though presumably all leading to the same ultimate goal. The truth of the matter is that the answers to the riddle of the phenomenon of Pleasura are not simply "A" or "B," "black" or "white"; there are also gradations of each and various shades of grey.

In terms of blood and race, if we look at the struggle between blacks and whites in South Africa during the spring of 1990, we are surprised to find the rule of "blood" being thwarted with respect to the expected unity-in-Pleasura, as it were, of the black race. One would have anticipated a common unity of black effort furthered and nurtured by "blood" slogans of unity—"brotherhood" and "sisterhood" and so on—as was evidenced by the black race in the United States in the decades of the 1960s and 1970s. But there is a difference.

In the United States modern blacks are descendants of mingled slaves of assorted tribes and groupings: the slave system in the United States did not logistically provide for tribal or other groups to remain intact demographically. The slaves were scattered to the winds by the men who bought them and who had no interest in the maintaining of elementary family units let alone tribal and other collective groupings. Therefore, the blacks in America today have no significant tribal memories or affiliations: their one element in common, other than the particular shade of black or brown they may be, is that they are all members of the black race.

Thus the rallying calls of the "blood" were easy and fortuitous Pleasura invocations for American blacks of the 1960s and 1970s. "Brothers," "sisters,"

fell easily off their lips and were accepted and acknowledged enthusias-
tically, heightened by the euphoria of the knowledge of new power and
freedoms that their collective "blood" group anticipated and demanded.
The superiority of the "blood" was vaunted as well; "Black is beautiful,"
and many variations of the "black is better," view are still invoked at
the altar of black Pleasura. In short, the American black civil liberty thrust
had the muscle and intensity behind it of a collective black Pleasura.

In the spring of 1990, Nelson Mandela, the publicized black anti-
Apartheid leader was released from prison in South Africa. For the ten
years of his incarceration he had been the acknowledged leader and certainly the symbol of collective South African black power.

It seemed that all the potentiality for an American "black-power" style
of Pleasura manifestation was present, only awaiting Mandela's release.
The black hatred of Apartheid laws, the common black acknowledgment
of universal racial suffering at the hands of Apartheid, stimulation and
encouragement from the Western press and the lionizing of other black
leaders and agitators such as Desmond Tutu had the effect of accentu-
ating the image and charisma of the yet-unfreed Mandela. It seemed that
all that the potential now required was the necessary prevailing circumstance of Mandela's release to ignite the collective black Pleasura like an
incendiary spark.

All of this was aided and abetted by the lessening of the ruling white
power's hold on the whip of terror. In the face of united world opinion, as well as political and economic sanctions, the quantum of white
Realitas terror was diminished to a shade less than the quantum of black
Pleasura actually manifested and in negative potential.

This brings into view a recent social phenomenon: external coercion upon
a given Realitas in order to diminish, in turn, the terror it imposes upon
its own or other groups. Collections of nations today come together
politically as a collective Realitas to impose and extend a portion of that
Realitas—pertaining to its substantial political thought and allegiances—
on other and presumably despotic Realitases.

For the purposes of this work, a despotic or intrinsically dangerous
Realitas (one that threatens the survival of others) can be referred to as
a "negative" Realitas. In effect, by this we mean a Realitas that is itself,
as an entity, in an ascendant state of Negative Pleasura and thereby is
in a state of criminality, if rule of law of the international grouping of
nations is assumed to be predicated on the categorical "Thou shalt not
do violence to nor cause danger to your neighbor."

The new collective Realitas by virtue of its function as sanctioner
of the collective rule of law, which was the original intention of the United

Nations, has now been effectively introduced internationally by the phenomenon of the Gulf War and has now established the precedent for sanction of the collective rule of law by economic and other measures, and
by force itself. Prior to these coercive remedies being put into effect, persuasion will no doubt come to be used, followed by sanctions and force.
This sort of persuasion by coercion as a tool to offset and correct the
threats of a dangerous Negative Realitas to the new collective rule of law
could be called "sanctuasion." It is here assumed that the survival Pleasura
instincts of nations, now having a precedent of effective action through
a collective Realitas, will seek to utilize that precedent in the future. The
practice is as old as ancient Rome itself: in times of objective external
danger, it submitted to interim dictators. It is hoped that that word will
perpetually maintain its historical caveats vis-à-vis the phenomenon of
collective Realitas as the imposer of ultimatums.

"Sanctuasion" is accomplished by appealing through coercion, e.g.,
sanctions imposed on the Negative Realitas's basic Pleasura thereby threatening its survival. By "coercion" here is meant external pressure of a forceful
and compelling nature but not necessarily violence. Any tactic that compels
the object of that tactic to respond favorably out of fear of some kind
(for example, through economic pressure) is for the purpose of this work
deemed coercion or "sanctuasion." "Sanctuasion" is therefore an arbitrary
classification to describe a form of persuasion related to coercion, be it
peaceful or if need be forceful.

The value question is here addressed lest improper valuation be affixed to the term "coercion." Digressing for a moment on this point, it
should be noted that "coercion" does have a positive value argument for
itself in the proper circumstances, as was the case in the 1991 Gulf War.
The question of value here is related to the prudential, to the practical.
The value label can be affixed by looking at the nature of those who
impose the coercion and their motivation. Related to motive assessment
is the "objective" test as to the value of that which is sought to be achieved
or avoided by the use of collective coercion. More and more groups of
nations, through the United Nations or other multinational organizations,
are seeking to further the "civilization" nature of the social environment.
They find themselves obligated to use their collective strength through the
"coercion" tactic of sanctuasion to persuade maverick despot rulers and
Negative Realitas groups from indulging in Negative Pleasura setbacks.
It is a form of persuasion, perhaps the only form understood by Negative
Pleasura or able to stop the violent brutish attack.

These collective coercive attempts will inevitably be met by the knee-
jerk "value-reactors," those who label actions negative in value solely because they are coercive. But the rule of law in democratic society is also

necessarily coercive. The fact that other alternatives do not seem available is not considered by these otherwise well-intentioned (Positive Pleasura) people who become mingled in the same resisting crowd with Negative Pleasura proponents and puppets: for example, friends and supporters of despots or malevolent discontents seeking to make political or other fodder out of the situation for their own narrow ends.

In the case of the Gulf War, the target was an international danger for which we had irrefutable evidence: i.e., the forceful seizure of a neighboring sovereign state, the assembling and production of weapons of mass-destruction, and a Negative Pleasura ruler at the helm of the Realitas with a will and intent to match. In practical terms, by virtue of the good fortune of Iraq not being a super-power, coercion was a practical expedient. The voices of the Western opponents were soon on the scene, loud and vocal, refusing to acknowledge (or perhaps truly not understanding) civilization's high stake in this particular "uncivilized" action of coercion. And there were political opportunists, those with Pleasura axes to grind, who by hint and by innuendo (invoking the familiar fears and hatreds known to Negative Pleasura) sought to scuddle the operation or at least to make political hay out of it.

Having said all that, one must add the caveat that sweeping "value" criticisms of forceful coercion must always have their due place in any situation where the use of coercion could lead to civilization's ends. Men are not infallible machines: human judgment, if for no other reason than a Pleasura survival one, must always be open to *reasonable* scrutiny in an objective and common-sense manner. It is not difficult for ordinary human beings, let alone experts, to examine the factual data and determine if the "end" of the coercion is justified in terms of particular survival (individual or collective) threats and thus in terms of civilization's progress and protection.

Humankind may slowly be on the way to a new phenomenon of "international" collective Realitas. However, such a Realitas, inasmuch as it does not arise from Pleasura of ethnicity, will always be a fragile one bound by the most fragile of threads, the ones of reason and logic. The emotional support for such a Realitas will be based on the hardy Pleasura standbys of survival: the collective Realitas association could produce, in the end, an international (as well as collective) freedom from insecurity and from threat of aggressive destruction.

Contemporary Western nations, believing in the ideals of human equality, have collectively, if informally, come to impose sanctions upon South Africa as a "coercion" method, threatening its economic survival—a Pleasura concern. This practice will, in the years to come, become more prevalent: the unified collective Realitas will in the natural course of things seek more and more to impose world orders of stability and the political ideals of equality and freedom. The sanction method was also applied to Iraq as a first coercive stage in the Gulf War. For puposes of international safety, sanctions may also be addressed more frequently as an expeditious safety measure to head off the steam of a particular Negative Realitas.

Nelson Mandela's release sparked substantial black enthusiasm, as a whole, but not the blind, frenzied black adulation and mass, blindly obedient following and support that the conventional wisdom might have expected. Many young African blacks have not flocked to his embrace but have rather examined him more closely as a man than as a charismatic idol and in many ways have found him wanting due to the human deficiencies of age and its weaknesses, including a perceived mellowing. The great charismatic "blood" leader has been treated as another, though greater, black man but a man after all.

Further, an unexpected concomitant phenomenon has occurred since his release. Rather than exhibiting a universal black unity in a massive manifestation of black Pleasura, the bizarre phenomenon of violent black divisiveness has manifested itself. In the second week of April 1990 alone, ten black deaths were reported as part of the inter-black restlessness and hostility. The news reports and commentaries informed us that the rivalries were intertribal and concerned territorial disputes. Tribal rivalry and dispute is not an unknown factor in the black situation in South Africa. The Zulu tribes of the north are inimical to the tribes comprising the African National Congress Association.

The black tribe has become for Pleasura purposes a blood-within-blood. Pleasura always takes the most selfish view, the meanest view, the narrowest view, for this is the essence of Pleasura, the self and its welfare as the primal consideration. And the mean view being the least sophisticated view, the self (in terms of groups) that is easiest for the individual to identify with is the most compact "self" (in terms of the group of which he is a part). It is harder to identify, in Pleasura terms, with the wider and more dissociated group or combination of groups to which an individual may loosely belong. Like water seeking its own level, the "self"-craving impulse (the Pleasura impulse) to identify with a group body in order to be a living part of it finds its home in the closest and most accessible niche, the smallest, most compact group to which it is "related." Stepping one up from the family, there is the tribe.

Thus, in the face of Pleasura reality manifested in tribal personas mass black Pleasura is unable to wholly prevail. The Pleasura outcroppings of countervailing eruptions are manifested in black (in terms of "tribal") versus black, in spite of all the exhortations to the contrary by Mandela. In pre-white North America, Indian tribes would raid each other from time to time in deadly attacks though they were all of the same racial blood: territorially they differed.

With the loss of tribal memory and association, American black Pleasura was able to prevail as a unifying force, welding the mass of black opinion and sentiment into a unified whole, feeling and expressing rage and Pleasura-inspired craving for power for the black "self." This phenomenon exhibited the characteristic classical Pleasura invocations, as we have seen the brother-sister appellations (ever rising above this worldly space to experience a sort of divine blood relationship, as in "soul" brother and "soul" sister). What was lacking to fuel the black Pleasura to high intensity was the factor of territory, i.e., a designated "motherland" or "fatherland."

But "territory" was not really part of the American black Pleasura claim. Rather, it was advocating a vast enlargement of its hitherto limited power (a national Pleasura goal), under the mantle of seeking civil rights. It was an angry, embittered Pleasura, choking with bile at long and recent memory of almost total domination under white power.

Territory was not part of the black Pleasura mandate in that blacks generally

(1) don't seek to return to Africa—on the contrary; and
(2) no territory within the geographic United States is so exclusively black or significant to blacks that they see it as their native country within the geopolitical boundaries of the United States. Rather, American blacks share the same "sentimental" homeland as the whites, namely, the predominantly white homeland, the territorial United States.

Thus, in the absence of a "This-is-our-land-not-yours!" cause, a potential great blood bath was averted. The American Black Movement in the main, under the sound leadership of Martin Luther King, Jr., shunned violence and found its place in the sun through dialogue, though often sprinkled with black blood during those days, including the blood of King himself.

India witnessed a peaceful transition even though the "This-is-our-land-not-yours!" invocation was available. The reason is twofold:

(1) Mahatma Gandhi's policy of nonviolence. Only Gandhi, the charismatic embodiment of Indian Pleasura, could have exerted the necessary influence to restrain the Pleasura eruption. This he did but it was only a matter of time before it burst forth.

This leads to the next reason:

(2) The recognition by the British of the inevitable reality of mass, violent confrontation and their subsequent cool-headed strategy and good sense to withdraw in time.

The result of a decision not to withdraw would have been disastrous at that time:

England, so soon after the war, lacked the physical capability and perhaps more important, the will to impress and perpetuate its Realitas position in the only manner that would have been left open to it, namely, imposing terror on the colony in a prolonged, massive occupation and a show of force that would offset the already considerable quantum of Indian Pleasura.

Furthermore, England was in the new and uncomfortable position of having to confront the rising Pleasura of a United States that was feeling its oats after the victories of World War II and was determined to impress its influence, ideas, and power internationally. Part of America's ideological approach then, as now, was to see colonialism end and former colonies achieve independence. In its own Pleasura of pride of victory and newfound international strength, it was now a matter of both Negative and Positive Pleasura to promote policies of anti-colonialism, negative in that it represented the imposition by the U.S. of its influence upon others, and positive in that the end philosophy of what it was promoting was a product of the positive, freedom for the colonized.

Winston Churchill, one of the last great manifestations of English Pleasura, had been determined to see the British Empire survive the war intact. Franklin Roosevelt and the United States, however, foresaw a different state of affairs. Not to withdraw from India under the circumstances would have been imprudent and embarrassing for Britain when the final, inevitable backdown in the face of American pressure would have occurred.

Britain's colonial policy was in this manner perhaps the first subject of modern collective Realitas will to impose a view of order upon the world at large. The instrument of this collective Realitas was to be, of course, the United Nations, which F.D.R. promoted and which came into being in San Francisco in the last days of the war. Paradoxically, we find an elementary Pleasura root cause in the formation of the United Nations, namely, "survival." That is, the Second World War showed leaders like Roosevelt just how vast and devastating the scope of future wars would be, even to the survival of the United States itself. (This latter point was especially relevant in light of the development of nuclear weapons.)

Tribal Pleasura is a "blood" Pleasura, in the final analysis, but a territorial one as well. It is a "blood-within-the-blood," or "territory-within-the-territory" Pleasura, convincing its participants that the part is greater than the whole, at least in terms of ultimate emotional significance. The more general and disjointed the grouping structure, the more difficult the Pleasura task than that of the sort which arises out of a unified whole with all its concomitant strength and energy. This holds except for extraordinary circumstances, such as a threatened crisis; threatening the substantial safety and territorial integrity of the whole, it is a crisis so tangible and material that each individual perceives it as relating to himself in a sense of highly personal urgency and danger of the sort (whatever that may be) that causes him to identify with the overall group itself in priority to personal and even tribal considerations. The United States during the Second World War was subject to those conditions and its Pleasura responded accordingly. That sense of personal crisis and urgency was absent in the Vietnam confrontation.

Thus it would be a highly unlikely scenario for the Caucasian race as a whole to be stirred to rise as a whole against any other race. Rather, the fortified intertribal pattern of confrontation that has characterized the situation of the Caucasian race divided against itself throughout history seems most likely to continue and to perpetuate itself. Universalism is a bar to equivalent Pleasura. It is too hard to identify with the universal. Pan-Arabism, for example, is too universal a thesis, as witness the continuing conflict among Arab interests. Pleasura is a natural creature, and no amount of pressure or artificial structuring will fool the phenomenon of Pleasura: it has been around longer than modern propagandists.

It is Pleasura that drove Saddam Hussein into Kuwait to seize and engulf it, notwithstanding its Arabness. It is Pleasura—elementary survival fear—that impelled conservative Saudi Arabia to join the "coalition" collective Realitas. It is the Pleasura of needed, reaffirmed national self-esteem of America after the Vietnam debacle that reflected its gratitude to the administration of President Bush. It is a new phenomenon (reflecting the disappearance of East-West survival fears), a more universal, international survival Pleasura, that impelled the many and diverse nations to join and/or support the collective effort against Saddam Hussein and in the effort, to set a precedent.

Since the Gulf War, the long-festering ethnic rivalries of the former Yugoslavia have erupted in severe and vicious hostilities betwen Serbs and Croats. The blood-letting in Bosnia-Herzegovina has led to an outcry for a similar military expeditionary incursion into the region, but this has not been forthcoming. It is worthwhile at this point to examine several relevant issues.

First, like the former Soviet Union and Yugoslavia, Czechoslovakia has split apart, but into two states, Czech and Slovak. What it shares in common with Yugoslavia is that there is an uncertainty as to whether the masses of the respective populations really assented prior to their leaders taking the fateful steps. In Czechoslovakia, a democracy, the empowered leaders acted suddenly—and possibly to the economic detriment of both parties. In Yugoslavia, Serbs and Croats lived in relative, blood-free harmony notwithstanding submerged tension. The Pleasura of necessity and survival could have maintained the greater whole in a precarious harmony until long-term political solutions could be found. But the leaders acted with dispatch, perhaps too much dispatch. One must question whether Negative Pleasura, ethnic pride, "blood," and so on, did not push these leaders into their actions. Czechoslovakia is peaceful. With the cessation of Yugoslavian dialogue at the table, however, the tragic blood bath began: the usual Negative Pleasura human slaughterhouse ritual in tribute to its insatiable appetite for human blood. Perhaps Pleasura of survival must needs dictate a restriction on the power of leaders, even democratically elected ones, to have the authority to bind countries (again, the power of the one over the millions) on such crucial questions without a national vote wherein the Pleasura of survival of the many might, just possibly, outflank the Negative but heady Pleasura of the few.

But to return to Yugoslavia and the lack of military incursion, two Pleasuras are here in question. First, the Pleasura of survival (in a limited sense at least) will always play a part in future decisions for a "Desert Storm"-type operations. The participants will ask themselves, as does the United States now concerning the former Yugoslavia: could this be, for example, another Vietnam? Unlike Kuwait, this is something of an internal mess, not a clear act of external aggression lending itself to a neat, surgical thrust and departure. Here guerrilla warfare can well be anticipated, and with the Serbian success in the resistance during World War II, the prospect is not inviting. This is reality. Pleasura self-interest will, of necessity, be a controlling influence in "Desert Storm"-type decisions. Second, the Positive Pleasura aspect must be clear. External aggression is clear and unequivocal. Here, though rampant cruelty and human tragedy is abundantly clear, the issue is not as clear-cut as the case of external aggression: a type of civil war tragedy seems more of the nature of the hostile operations in former Yugoslavia. Where doubt exists, Positive Pleasura is not quick to act by force.

10

China and Russia

(As a result of the continuing upheaval in China since June 5, 1989, these notes, as a matter of interest, were compiled during the uprising and before its final outcome. They are offered as jotted down from time to time during those days.)

Earlier I had surmised that the Chinese students' "demonstration" would result in a tapering off of enthusiasm and fervor on the part of the demonstrators, leading to disintegration of the revolt. That is, I had postulated that the Realitas leadership, namely, the government in power, would rest on its laurels of former terror remembered, wait things out, and survive.

However, at this date, the government in power seems to have miscalculated the danger that the demonstrating students pose. That is, they do not seem to understand that there is no one leader, there is no one unifying and particular bond to open forth the channels of Negative Pleasura: rather, there are the more general Pleasura principles of "democracy" and "corruption" being invoked. So long as this general situation holds (and nothing more), the prevailing government is in no danger; it can continue to negotiate, bide its time, and wait for this generation to grow out into the realities of poststudent idealism.

As a result of overestimating the "conflagration" potential of this student Pleasura, the government has gone through a brief, indecisive period. Unsure of itself, it has made conciliatory signals to the student organizers and there have been meetings with them. This period of equivocation within the Realitas seems now to be over. It has finally decided that the necessary element of terror must be reinforced, and it has sent in troops. However, those troops have overreacted, killing some 3,000 students if reports are accurate.

This could be the necessary ingredient binding those student (and supporter) forces opposed to the government into a more Negative Pleasura state. At present, there still does not seem to be that necessary Negative Pleasura unifier, save and except for the enormous indignation arising on the part of the students by virtue of the slaughter of their "own." The threads of unification in the opposing groups are thus being tied more closely together.

The next step must be that leaders personifying a oneness of the group must arise. Further, the indignation and hurt must be so deeply and seriously felt that in fact the diverse categories of individuals forming the students and their outside supporters, but most certainly the group of students itself, must see itself as a unified cadre of a "oneness," a brotherhood, a "blood" group to actualize the potential for Negative Pleasura that presently exists.

That is, the necessary prevailing circumstances must come together. At present, the initial components of necessary prevailing circumstances seem to be gathering themselves. But not all of the necessary elements are yet there.

(Excerpt of further notes made during the Chinese uprising:)

Looking at the progression of the "uprising" some two weeks after the shooting of the students, one finds two of the necessary prevailing elements offering themselves to the potential Negative Pleasura. Personification of the group into one leader in the person of a dissident student who is seeking sanctuary in the American Embassy in Beijing. However, it is doubtful whether he is widely known to be the necessary personification that the requisite leader would have to possess. Second, as to the questions of the "blood" issue: this week, the third week, a slogan is now generating among the dissident students both in China and abroad to the effect that "the blood must not be forgotten," speaking about the bloodshed by the students who were shot by the soldiers. However, once again, it does not seem to have pinpointed itself into a unified invocation with both strength and immediacy. The Realitas regime seems to have reinstated itself forcefully through terror. To checkmate the uprising, the government-controlled television programs show the populace buckling under, sisters informing on their dissident brothers, soldiers being praised, etc. Foreign journalists are now turned away where once they were welcomed. That is, the policy of reinstatement of terror is taking effect, and the Realitas force manifested in the present Chinese government is digging itself in with greater stability.

This leads to the conclusion that the winner of the two forces in any dialectical confrontation between them can be determined by the extent to which one exceeds the other. That is, if the amount of terror (and here we are speaking effective terror of the sort that made the populace buckle under) exceeds the amount of the Negative Pleasura force, the Realitas will dominate: and vice versa. This appears to be the situation at present in China. The prediction can therefore be made that the effects of the revolt will not be offering a threat to the stability of the present Realitas regime: the seeds for a future Negative Pleasura may well have been sown, but again those seeds remain potential to be cast into the future and will develop only if the necessary fertile ground is there. Furthermore, the seeds themselves must be strong enough to "take," even if the ground is fertile. That was not the case in the present "uprising."

For Negative Pleasura to be effective, the means of insurrection must be available as a necessary prevailing condition: the guns, ammunition, etc. These were lacking and as a result there was less injury inflicted on the greatly outnumbered students. Escalated violence would have drawn them still closer into a "blood" cause. The absence of weapons in the hands of the people is very obviously a stabilizing factor in favor of the perpetuation of the Realitas regime then in power. That regime whether totalitarian or "free" which lulls itself into thinking that because of its present and foreseeable strength it need not fear arms in the hands of its people, is sowing the seeds of its own destruction.

We should note that the importance to Negative Pleasura of available weaponry in the hands of the people is so obvious that even the remote possibility of a consensus against such availability represents danger of the first order. A people in Pleasura lacking weaponry is like a pit bull at a dog fight with all its teeth extracted. Pleasura is skillfully devious: it clothes the subject of weaponry in the robes of Positive Pleasura—i.e., freedom, rights, survival, etc.—so that one of its favorite defensive methods is successful again, i.e., the method of "turning the tables." Thus the subject of weapon availability finds fewer overwhelming detractors and critics as vociferous supporters and adherents in numberless abundance decry criticism of weapon availability as attacks upon basic freedoms and rights. This is vintage Negative Pleasura—shrewd manipulation.

The greatest catastrophe of the twentieth century is the vast distribution and availability of weaponry and ammunition, especially to what we know as underdeveloped countries. It is akin to the contacting of "backward" groups and peoples and infecting them with deadly germs and viruses. It is like the decimation of native populations of Eskimos or Amazon Indians, for example, by the white man's germs of the common cold, mumps, etc. However, there is one difference here from our example: in the case of weaponry the effects of the disease do not merely incapacitate the "infected" groups, they radiate outward with all the vitality of radio-wave transmission to the rest of the world, compromising its general security and crippling its capability to progress onward through the signposts of civilization along the endless road to human self-realization.

Pleasura rejoices in this: once again for expediency we slip into the imagery of Pleasura as some great transcending rational and devious material presence that is able to manipulate and control us. In fact the manipulation and control part is true, but the Pleasura is individually housed in each of us, though its individual general potentialities, especially for negative excesses, are mostly manifested through the vehicle of the group. There is no external Pleasura puppeteer pulling all the strings, but rather millions of duplicate puppeteers within millions of psyches pulling the same strings and able to work in concert within groups, resulting in a group psyche Pleasura. So long as there is one uncontrolled gun with one bullet out there, Negative Pleasura always has at the ready at least one potential match to ignite perhaps the last and greatest Negative Pleasura holocaust, one not even wished for by Pleasura itself, which seeks in the end to survive its own death-defying orgies.

The wide dissemination of weaponry is, in the case of each single weapon, like a time delay. We are not just talking of caches of pistols and rifles; we refer to the outfitting of entire armies, navies, and air forces with the most modern and sophisticated weaponry and technology. This will seem in the judgment of future historians of our species to have been one of the grossest and most remarkable cases of recklessness in the general administration of human affairs.

A people who seek the "right" to possess and carry arms as a "constitutional" and/or "democratic" right, as a "tenet of freedom," etc., is a people expressing its latent Negative Pleasura need for future "insurance." Its future "insurance" is the ready availability of arms. Pleasura is patient: it bides its time, though that time may appear endless. And like the slogan of the British navy, when the opportunity finally arises, it will reply "Ready, aye ready!" Especially so with arms at hand.

Another necessary circumstance working hand-in-hand with the unity of the Negative Pleasura group is the need to communicate the message. There must be time enough and adequate access and means for a communication of the Negative Pleasura within the oppressed of that nation to be spread throughout. In the recent upheaval in China, there was a very short period of time—mere weeks—within which all of this happened. And as we have observed, there were no really adequate means of communication of what was going on for the messages of the dissidents to be spread throughout the outer regions of China where the masses (80 percent) live.

The Realitas group controlled, as it does today, the means of communication. It has now "educated" the 80 percent in the outlying areas, through its own messages, that the upheavals were the result of wrong-doers, bent at harming the public interest, and so on. This seems to have been met with significant acceptance thus far by the Chinese public, there-by further mitigating against the formation of a united dissident group against the ruling Realitas. However, as we have observed, a Realitas is subject to its own Pleasura of survival. Having, in this regard, recognized the tip of a possible emerging Pleasura spear in the hands of the ruled, the Realitas regime will seek to deflect its thrust, to dull its edge in practi-cal fashion: it will no doubt address the acceleration of the process of opening the trade door even more to the West. In this regard, one can envisage great leaps forward in experimentation with a market economy, but all of this within an ever-tighter, if more diplomatic mailed fist.

With regard to the terror presently being employed by the Realitas group in China, some days after the foregoing observations were written, an article appeared in the *Toronto Star* on June 19, 1989, on page D1, with the title "China Takes Great Leap Backwards Into Terror." The title of that article concisely sums up the strategy of the Realitas regime to preserve itself.

The Realitas has many strategies in its determination for self-preservation. Its prime tool is its flexibility when the need arises, a paradox consider-ing the apparent inflexibility of entrenched Realitas regimes, but under-standable in light of the fact that a Realitas, like a person, is subject to its own Pleasura of survival, and guided by it.

For example, in the Second World War, Josef Stalin was caught nap-ping by Hitler. In spite of his own intelligence reports, Stalin refused to believe that Hitler would breach the nonaggression pact Germany had signed with Russia and which had resulted in the "friendly" division of Poland. Hitler disappointed Stalin and invaded Russia. Stalin was shaken and disappeared behind the walls of his country dacha for five days. Presum-ably, he was letting the shock set in, adjusting to it. Stalin was the consum-mate dictator, unafraid to lavish terror on his subjects and firm in his opposition to institutions and ideas contrary to the interest of the ruling Realitas, which was in fact Stalin himself. Such institutions were deemed to be pitting themselves, euphemistically, against the "interests of Com-munism." Foremost among these adverse institutions was the church.

When Stalin emerged finally from his dacha, he broadcast a radio message to his people. As we noted earlier, he began with the three words he had never used before (though they are a common Russian greeting), "Brothers and Sisters." He called back into service the formerly deposed clergy and religion was suddenly once more tolerated. And he spoke of the need to defend the "Motherland." He was transforming himself into the requisite Pleasura symbol, "Brother-Comrade Stalin," and he was invoking the survival Pleasura then rising in the hearts of the people who faced the very real danger of German attack.

The Nazi attack was the necessary prevailing circumstance for the eruption outward of the pent-up Russian Negative Pleasura (now surmounted by Pleasura of national survival): all that the masses' Pleasura now required was a symbolic Pleasura leadership, and this Stalin offered them in his own person. His hated ruthlessness and strength were now welcomed by a needy and besieged people: if Stalin was their "brother" and "comrade," his strength and force would be theirs, and they would prevail. Thus a subject people's Pleasura formerly trampled by Stalin is let loose from its irons to be led into battle by its former captor, now its captain and beloved leader. So successful was this formerly hated leader that the defending Russians threw themselves bodily against the oncoming German tanks shouting "Stalin!" The Russian nation, formerly a group in the hold of an internally resented Realitas, was momentarily and instantaneously transformed into a group manifesting national Pleasura against an external threat. That is how quickly the turnabout can happen given the proper circumstances. Pleasura is unable to fight a war on two fronts at the same time: i.e., against the Realitas and as well against a real or perceived group enemy (whether internal or external).

Post Communist Russia and Eastern Europe

The exquisite suddenness of the Soviet disintegration is a fair cause for wonder but not the disintegration itself. The most basic cry of Pleasura, economic privation, has finally felled the Communist Realitas in Russia and eastern Europe. This process is as inevitable as condensation producing a liquid. Notwithstanding the repressive measures of the ruling Realitas, the basic Pleasura of necessity will, if unrequited, prevail in time either violently or otherwise. In a battle of endurance between the will of Realitas to maintain itself by terror and the will of Pleasura of necessity (and even of peripheral Pleasura of desire), the will of Pleasura will win out in the end.

The decline of the Roman Empire was aided and abetted by a passive willingness of an impoverished and disaffected people. Exploited by the shortsighted meanness of the small group of vast landowners and owners of the bulk of the wealth who comprised the backbone of the Realitas—albeit a sliding and failing one—the populace had no will to stand up to the barbarians and defend their native land. The Roman Pleasura was one of unsatisfied necessity fueled by duress and economic oppression, preempting Pleasuras of patriotism, blood, etc. Its will may not have been to rise up and overthrow the Realitas, but neither was it to stand up to and fight off the barbarian (who indeed might have meant a change for the better). Again, we must have recourse to our well-used analogy of the former Soviet Union. In the face of the reality of insolvency so vast that the cosmetic of armed might could no longer veil it, the will of the Soviet Union to "keep its doors open for business" as it were, finally and suddenly disintegrated and the receivers and trustees were called in to oversee its break-up. It had managed to maintain its facade of confidence to a suspecting but unsure external world for an abnormally long time. But in the end it was felled by economic reality, as had been the case with revolutionary France. Where there had been a governing Realitas one day, the very next there was none (unless we count a bankrupt and impotent vestige).

The student of social-psychological history will, if sympathetic to the general goal of human self-realization, view with alarm a vacuum left in a culture by the sudden elimination of Realitas. Pleasura seeks to occupy a social vacuum. This is especially true if that vacuum was (1) preceded by dissatisfaction (as in Russia and eastern Europe) and (2) if those same prevailing Pleasura-igniting conditions are still substantially in place and remain unaddressed. The Russian people will be equally alarmed and perturbed if what they would deem "responsible forces" do not proceed with a plan for reconstruction of the wounded social system, primarily the economic wounds. The stakes are not national or ethnic or political only; they are in historical terms universal.

In the case of Russia and eastern Europe, one fact to consider is the attendant additional gap in the expertise required for a remedial and inspired program of reconstruction. This gap in the body social is an irresistible attraction to the forces of Pleasura generally. Pleasura, like existence itself, will fill every nook and crevice that is open to it, submitting only to the limitations of its own energy and to any Realitas's external controls. The problem is that Pleasura includes as a fundamental part of its makeup its dormant negative phase which only awaits arousal. Prophylactic social measures are called for in such circumstances if the negative portion of Pleasura is not, like some evil genie, to be called forth from its bottle.

A compelling historical parallel can be found in the Peace Conference of 1919 after the First World War. This was also a time of political reconstruction of an old ethnic-riddled and ruined world. It was a golden opportunity for the building of a secure Realitas upon which the various incompatible national and ethnic Pleasuras could rest secure, if not happy in their mutual new alignments together, at least settling into a practical acceptance of the compromises of togetherness. This new unity presumably would have been molded into place by an ever-hardening mortar of basic practicality of planned economy and politics. In the words of one observer, the Europe of the Peace Conference was "as clay ready for the creative potter." Just so is the world of the former socialist regimes of eastern Europe.

That the clay was not creatively molded is proven by the Second World War (and the subsequent postwar discord that exists to this day). Once again clay is available for the potters, but are the potters available or inclined to the task? Perhaps there is no necessity in the perpetuation of the human race or in its reasonable improvement toward a goal of self-realization. However, such necessity seems compelling to a rational mind alerted to the wonders of the infinite potentialities of matter and the limitless potentialities of reasonable people.

That is, if a philosophy of general Positive Pleasura were to be posited, one propounding progress to the "higher ideals," the "end good," of human self-realization, this opportunity to attempt a stable social base economically and politically in eastern Europe will be attractive. If, however, the individual national and ethnic Pleasuras of both the West and the constituent former participants of the Soviet Union and its satellites predominate over the Positive Pleasura, then the eastern European situation will be allowed to fall into the clutches of Negative Pleasura, for such will undoubtedly be the case, as is already being witnessed.

The vacuum of power and economic stability invites in the proven economic system of capitalist free enterprise, a relatively constructive system, all things being equal. An abdication of a longstanding Realitas does not also mean a sudden extinguishing of all its attendant ideas. A strong Realitas, such as the Soviet Union was, imposes its own kind of culture onto the ruled. Values, images, ways, and means are influenced by the strong Realitas, if not explicitly then subtly. Russia is especially vulnerable to certain Western "corrupting" influences because of this. The Russian concept of "freedom" under the Communist regime was not of a war-free world but of a world ruled entirely by Communism. Travelers returning from the Ukraine report that in the main people don't understand democracy: they think it gives them the freedom to do anything they want. Perhaps partially, as a result, there has been a concurrent one-third rise in the crime rate since the institution of *glasnost*. Further "freedom," an especially deadly word to a totalitarian Realitas regime, was given its Negative-Pleasura contextual meaning by the former Soviet rulers and was seen as the ability to be as corrupt and as criminal as one pleases. Now suddenly this negative value is elevated as the goal to be sought after if one is to live in a Western-style free market society. The Negative Pleasura influences could be stifled through all this if the situation generally had some solid supporting social substructure.

External to Russia and eastern Europe we have a situation akin to that of the nations who attended the Peace Conference of World War I, a situation comprised of nations encumbered by their own economic problems and preoccupations and unable to unfetter the blinders of their own national selfish Pleasura considerations to expend energy and resources on reconstruction. Such blinders represent a fatal shortsightedness, for indeed the best and securest means of safeguarding a nation's interest is to secure the international stability. Negative Pleasura fears international stability and seeks to discourage it by narrowing groups' legitimate Pleasura interest to limted personal contexts. The Peace Conference of 1919 failed because of this national nearsightedness and its concomitant lack of national wills. It degenerated into the mocking cynicism of Clemenceau jesting of Wilson's "14 points" that he had outdone the Lord who had only ten to give to Moses.

The same situation is presently being repeated by the West in eastern Europe. First of all, national economic problems as precipitated by the recession are being used to rationalize the nonheroic financial help needed by eastern Europe in its disastrous economic plight. It may thus degenerate into something wild and crouching, waiting, haunched on its flanks to spring and grab and tear, or indeed to be ensnared by some overpowering new master who will feed, control, and command it. Its fangs are sharp and radioactive. Its will is being corroded by hunger, humiliation, and despair. Its innate violence is being fueled by anger. Only selfish "unselfishness" (i.e., *prima facie* unselfish "help" given for the most selfish of reasons, one's own long-term survival) in the form of massive bridging economic help (without requiring iron-clad "business-like" guarantees of one kind or another) must be administered to the patient in this, its hour of mortal sickness.

In effect, the practical reasons so clearly and often enunciated by the West for not delivering more massive aid to Russia and eastern Europe may be nothing more than self-justifying rationalizations for a Negative Pleasura Western reaction. That is, the cold war has been in every other sense a real war, psychologically, morally, materially. And the fall of the Soviet Union, though peaceably, is no less a victory of war for the West than if it had been obtained through battle. The West is therefore as much in the position of victor in relation to the former Soviet Union as any previous conqueror. All that is lacking is the Negative Pleasura mainstream of bugles of victory, cries of delight of the conquerors, and of course, an abundance of blood. But this lack of the traditional accoutrements of victory have anesthetized the conqueror and dulled its consciousness to the reality of the situation. But its unconscious senses are alert and reacting.

In reality, the situation is as much one of terms of surrender as relevant as any conference after the victory. The vengeance-seeking quality of Negative Pleasura's demands compels, as in the unreasoning atmosphere after World War I, harsh conditions and reparations from the conquered. Unconsciously this is being reflected in the only way available to satisfy this vengeance-lusting of Negative Pleasura, and that is by the withholding of requisite, realistic massive aid (as for example was accomplished by the Marshall Plan after World War II). If I am correct in this assessment, the demands of Negative Pleasura in the foregoing respect are so very strong (no doubt as a result of the many years of tension and insecurity of the cold war) that they outweigh even the compelling requirements of basic survival Pleasura, i.e., that in the interests of the West's survival security a sound and stable reconstructed eastern Europe is vital. Once again, "Voe Victus" echoes through the drafty halls of the conquered.

Another consideration arises with regard to reconstruction. The naive recipient of the benefits of our capitalist free-enterprise system must be shielded from the evils of that same system to which seventy years of isolation from economic reality will have made eastern Europe vulnerable. There is an overriding moral and pragmatic responsibility to protect the naive believer from those abusers who naturally spring up within the environment of such a system because they are a potential (and early) manifestation of that system (in the absence of proven, realistic, and reasonable safeguards). These safeguards must be delivered along with the system, just as manuals of safety and other cautionary guidelines are delivered with nuclear energy systems to countries purchasing them from us.

The rationale for delivering caveats with the free-enterprise system is this: what good is their acceptance of the wine of our free-enterprise system if their vessel to contain it has holes in it or is of such a material that it will corrode and indeed poison the very wine that is to be drunk? Instead of having partners in free enterprise to build a greater international prosperity and harmony, the West will find itself with a strangled victim on its hands, one in tow by charlatans and demagogues: a dangerous victim with pockets full of radioactive weapons, one who is drugged, poisoned, embittered, and ready to do its masters' bidding, seeking the secure haven of the obedience side of the Realitas coin. This is not to say that one should fall prey to ever-constant naivete and believe that a solidly reconstructed eastern Europe is fail-proof against the manifestations of Negative Pleasura. Of course such a hypothesis is naive based as it is upon faulty logic, namely, that humans are somehow able to shake loose from the ever-present fetters of Negative Pleasura. But naivete and the reasonable taking of insurance against the outbreak of such phenomena are two entirely different things.

Implicit in the dangers outlined above is the cultural predisposition of the masses in the former Soviet Union to strong rule. Habit is a corrosive device relied upon by Negative Pleasura to eat into the will and moral fabric of a target people. When a habitual attitude is perpetuated over time it often seems to render the unacceptable acceptable, even desirable. In the Old Testament, after finally being liberated from the bondage of the Pharaohs, when the going got tough in the wilderness, the "Children of Israel" called out for the fleshpots of Egypt again. The former Soviet masses are now caught up in their own forty years in the wilderness. The going is tough. These are the peoples who have been ruled by despots and authoritarians for centuries. Negative Pleasura, seeking to reside in a protective citadel embracing authoritarianism, uses economic difficulty and privation as the colored lenses through which the suffering masses look to despotism with nostalgic longing. It enhances the view still more by filtering the light entering the lenses through the impulse of the desire-to-be-ruled side of Realitas. The cry for the fleshpots will always be under the surface. Perhaps an open democratic system is being too suddenly thrust upon these masses, so long used to its opposite, and now through economic privations looking back to it. Perhaps a new hybrid of democracy, one with a strong, authoritative nature—i.e., stronger than Western-style democracy—is here called for (if this would not be to embrace a contradiction). Perhaps simply a very strong (but free!) federal system is in order.

There is a question of priorities in addressing the Pleasuras. The first priority is the private Pleasuras of the individuals comprising the people of Russia and eastern Europe: in the face of Pleasura-invoking continued privation, the resulting resentment and despair must render the masses less than enthusiastic or supportive in the necessarily difficult and lengthy program of reconstruction of an entire economical and political system. Alleviating the "necessity" ordeal of the Russian and Soviet masses becomes a matter of primary importance under this mode of thinking.

Therefore it is essential to install (as well as instill) a capitalist system but (1) one that will work and (2) one that is immediate, as well as feasible, to act as a bridge between the dissolution of the old and the installation of a (permanent) new system. The highly impractical as well as unimaginative Communist-Socialist system has brought to bear once again an economic environmental crisis, this time as a result of its legacy of sterile productivity. After the Bolshevik Revolution of 1917 economic chaos and disorder quickly manifested themselves because the Communist-Socialist revolutionaries had omitted or (more likely) were incapable of planning for a working postrevolutionary economic system. The result: the revolution left in its wake an economic wasteland of distress upon an already unhappy people. Now in the post Communist-Socialist regime and system, Russia and the former Soviet Union have been left once again bereft of any practical interim economic system, let alone effective organizers or administrators. This vacuum must quickly be filled with remedial action.

The other concurrent initial agenda is the problem we have touched on above, namely, that of the ruthless pirates feeding on the natural misfortune of the infant free-enterprise system. Those who cannot protect themselves must be protected at the outset at least. The benefit of the West's business experience and regulatory expertise must be brought to bear to regulate, prohibit, expel, and/or punish these ruthless natural outgrowths of the system. In the alternative, there may be added to the misery of the masses the additional afflictions of buccaneering resulting in new Pleasura-invoking pain and disillusion. The West can handle these types and has indeed devised all sorts of measures to do so: however, it is too much to ask of naive capitalists.

The only historical and psychological legacy the Bolsheviks have left with regard to dealing with economic crises, especially at the outset of the installation of a Realitas, is terror. The postrevolution saw its successful installation. The Stalinists employed the established terror to buttress a philosophically orthodox though economically impractical regime. This is a cultural problem to be faced in dealing with the realities of reconstruction. Terror has now become historically and recently insinuated into the psychological fabric of the culture to the extent that there may very well be, on the unconscious level, a potential acceptance of terror as a necessary resort to the installation of a replacement Realitas. This would be contained in the "will-to-be-ruled" side of the Realitas coin within the mass psyche. As we have seen, one of the psychological reactions of the masses is, in the words of the Czech president, a desire "to return to jail."

With regard to the real and continuing "problem" of terror, it is significant that initially it was in great part an outcome of (prevailing) dire necessity. That is, attendant upon the Bolsheviks' seizing of power was a tragic state of mass disorder and pillage. Peasants arose, burned, destroyed, and appropriated to themselves arbitrarily the property of others. The country was in a state of chaos and mass violent crimes. All this was aided and abetted by a returning, hungry, and disillusioned army of eight million men, many of whom turned into nothing better than bandits, rapists, and brigands. Firearms were freely available to all, even the most criminal and insane, and these armed individuals walked the streets at large. This was an extreme situation calling for extreme measures in terms of a Realitas putting an immediate firm lid on rapacious, out-of-control Pleasura. The Bolshevik regime addressed the problem with terror as the easiest and most immediate solution. It worked. As a result, this terror must be faced as a probable "acceptable" Realitas method within the mass social psyche.

It must also be remembered in this regard that concurrent with the advent of the Bolshevik regime there arose a unanimous Western hostility to it, partially of a violent nature resulting in military and other aggressive forays against the Soviet Union. This reactive aggressive Pleasura of the West was quite possibly the natural result of the grotesque call by the Bolsheviks for international uprisings in the West against the Western governments, again thereby demonstrating the inordinate naivete of the Communist-Socialist philosophy. The problem is that this state of affairs prevented a situation arising of the West (understanding that it was to its own benefit so to do) helping the Soviet Union by way of economic reconstruction. No such systemic reconstruction program was provided. Thus, the former ruthless czarist police system was in the main perpetuated under the new Bolshevik regime inasmuch as no system of reconstruction provided otherwise. The KGB system, as it was until recently, is always available for a renascence to its former totalitarian enforcement status if the opportunity arises. Why should it not? Like any other entrenched social organization, it has its own Pleasura, now bottled by the new Realitas, but probably ready to erupt again if the stopper is removed.

11

Conclusion

The perpetual external dialectic between Pleasura and Realitas is accompanied by the internal one between the positive and negative component parts of Pleasura itself. Both are of crucial importance to the perpetuation of the human species. But as to that goal, are we not compelled to inquire into the value or necessity of the survival of the human race? And is there possibly some other struggle going on within the human psyche, more subtly perhaps, of which the other dialectics are manifestations? The dialectic we have proposed is not a classical one in that it leads to no clear synthesis. First, there is the Pleasura; emerging from it is the Realitas. Thus Realitas and the ruled Pleasura group interact: the result may be the overthrow of the Realitas with the Pleasura group becoming the Realitas and vice versa. There is some synthesis, some absorption into the new Realitas by the conquering Pleasura, of elements of the old Realitas. But in the main, the struggle is primarily antithetical and ongoing until a Realitas is either strong enough through terror (as in autocracies) or popular entrenchment (as in democracies) to maintain a continued superiority of control over the Pleasura group. The other case of dialectic is that of the combined Realitas plus Pleasura as one group (a Realitas-controlled group), belligerent and in a state of Negative Pleasura, rising up to threaten and attack a neighboring group, which presumably is in a state of Realitas.

We have seen that there is and always will be a struggle between the Realitas as the ordering and governing principle and the Pleasura, as the volcanic stuff of life (both good and bad) which must be ordered, governed, sorted out, and built upon. And we have concluded that the Realitas has, like the ego from the id, emerged as a Pleasura concession to its innermost motivation, survival. One might be optimistic that, all

151

things being equal, the balance of the scale will, perhaps imperceptibly over time, be tipped in favor of the Realitas. And in that optimism, humankind will hope that the positive nature of Realitas will outweigh the human predisposition to totalitarianism.

We are not, however, naive in broadly labeling a Realitas as "good": Realitases themselves, as we have observed, range from negative to positive. Their qualities in this regard are much more easily discernible than are those of the multifaceted spectrum of Pleasura. Thus, a Realitas that itself exhibits Negative Pleasura tendencies is a Negative Realitas: included are totalitarianism and any of the range of tyrannical rules; Realitases that exhibit unwarranted aggressive tendencies and acts toward neighbors or others, such being Negative Pleasura manifestations; and even Realitases that become so internally weakened and demoralized that they head upon paths of pure license disguised as "rights" (this latter category is at present one of degree).

Freud concentrated on the continuing battle between the individual and the external environment especially in terms of its restrictions against the individual's libidinal impulses.* He articulated what could be an apology for Nietzsche, namely, that "primitive man was better off in knowing no restrictions of instinct." But humankind's instinctual restrictions must have been internally imposed from the outset. The evidence for this is quite simply that humans are still around today and did not perish at the primitive stage. If there had been no inner countervailing limitations on the instinct to aggression, all human beings would have eventually killed each other off in the primitive times when Pleasura only was rampant on a Realitas-free field. Pre-civilized humans must have therefore voluntarily imposed these prohibitions upon themselves either through reason (though no doubt it lacks persuasive strength in primitive pre-history) and/or because of a prevailing Positive Pleasura impulse within the cauldron of the primitive psyche.

And this leads us to consider the question of an inner dialectic between the polar opposites of the Pleasura spectrum. We have pointed out that our labeling of Pleasura as negative has been primarily an arbitrary one for the purposes of this treatise: any Pleasura related to force as a means of achieving its ends we categorized as negative. But we pointed out that that was not intended as a dual-purpose labeling, i.e., to include valuation as well. In that regard we observed that, historically, some Negative Pleasura has been positive in value, as in the overthrow of tyranny (that is, in the strictest sense of objective accuracy as to the particular identification

---

Civilization and Its Discontents.

of tyranny and is the strict sense of positive motivation of the Pleasura agents).

However, in commenting upon the inner dialectic of Positive versus Negative Pleasura, we are here talking about Negative Pleasura in a value sense as well in our definition: we are talking about the negativity of Brutus, that catalogue of Pleasura ills that makes humans "a wolf to man" in the sense of the ancient phrase referred to by Freud. We are assuming a negative value to such an attitude (though others might see the opposite and find, like Nietzsche, that here lies the human nobility). And included under that head are the list of the many ingredients comprising criminality, cruelty, ruthlessness, and insatiability.

H. G. Wells has spoken of the race of humans arising out of the unconsciousness of animals to a continuing racial self-consciousness. I believe this observation is apt: in the mists of primitive pre-history there must have been a time that human beings, in their pre-*Homo sapiens* stages lacked self-awareness. Like our fellow animals, we existed and were then like a bit of broken straw whirling on a great (and unconscious) flood-tide of untrammeled Pleasura. That turgid water has remained in us, that pool of Negative Pleasura splashes against our soul. Out of it rise the sprites and goblins to challenge and wrestle with the Positive Pleasura. The Negative Pleasura is, after all, the old animal unconsciousness within us seeking to rouse itself, to arise and revel in a conscious animal self-awareness, one that only we could accommodate. It seeks the dominion of Pan: to ride the wild stallions of impulse, unrestrained, and it has had and will have its eloquent and faithful supporters.

Set off against this is the countervailing force of positive Pleasura seeking, along with our survival, our betterment in terms of the absolute good of the ideal of human self-realization. Writing on Nietzsche in 1939, Martin Heidegger declared that "there is no longer any goal in and through which all the forces of the historical existence of peoples can cohere and in the direction of which they can develop."* Heidegger's goal no doubt represented the confrontations of the external world, the dogged continuing, warring struggle for supremacy "in which those who struggle excel, first the one then the other and in which the power for such excelling unfolds within them."†

That is not the struggle we speak of here. Our reference is to an internal struggle of a type the sincere theologians early sensed, but we are not talking theologically. The unfolding power to excel in brute force is the power of Negative Pleasura: the greatest conquest is its reduction

---

*Martin Heidegger, *Nietzsche,* New York, Harper Collins, 1991, p. 157.
†Ibid., p. 158.

to submission by Positive Pleasura. This is the continuing goal of our species' nature as it progresses through the stages of history to its own self-realization. We must always remember that so far as the face of time is concerned, we are barely removed from the caves. It is a wonder that our brutish instincts are as controlled to the degree that they are within such a relatively short time span. It is no wonder that the "regressionists" still sing the praises of Brutus.

Through it all, we continue and will our continuance, but so does every other creature. Why should man prevail? As a creature, we are a pitiful species of primate, unclothed by nature for exposure to the elements, wild in our instincts, basic animal in all of our parts and functions, and barely able to survive for any period of time without continual ingestion of nutrients and oxygen. If we are not disposed to cleanliness individually our uncleanness will make us as rank (and even more so than) our fellow animals. We grunt and sweat and exhibit all the tendencies and predispositions of our teeth-baring fellow animals. We are in the main mean and self-seeking. Why should this race of creatures survive?

The question is old and trite as are the many answers, even as ours may be. But that does not necessarily derogate from its truth, if truth it is.

Though we are by no means heroic beasts notwithstanding our misbegotten pretensions and delusions of grandeur, our situation is. Our analogy is to a minute ant calmly proceeding on its untroubled way with a burden the comparable size of two- or three-story building on its back. The puny primate man is that ant, the great enormousness he carries on his back being his mind. We overlook the miraculous paradox of what we are, where we could be going. We are a form of monkey, upright to be sure, but monkey nevertheless, and far more defenseless to the external world than our hairier relatives.

The point is that a precious, ever-new thing is contained within a primitive, and some would say unworthy, container. It is of course mind, for the individual is his mind as the species is the collective minds of the individuals. But the mind is not a free thing: it is tied with the same rope that it can use as a tool in the external world, the Pleasura. The mind's goal is to be free, to untie itself from its bands of the negative. It can never be entirely free, but progressively, through will, it can be freer. And in that progression our potential blossoming from mind unfolds. That is the argument in favor of the perpetuation of the species, namely, that thereby the limitless and unknown potential of our mind can be progressively realized, this realization being concurrently part and parcel of human self-realization.

By virtue of the fortuitous accumulation of biological factors leading to the uniqueness of the human mind (a happy accident perhaps), "ape-like" man may have become a necessary prevailing circumstance for the manifestation of the mental process potential within matter. Matter thinks in humans. We are not here talking of the "purpose" to our existence but of an essential quality of it. Through no positive act of our own, we may have providentially become one of matter's instruments for self-awareness. As such, there are no limits to where destiny may carry our minds and spirits, no avenues within the great, limitless, and unfolding adventure of existence that our species may not tread. There are no heights of nobility and freedom to which our spirits cannot aspire as they unfold and blossom out within the radiance of self-realization. And the adventure of it all, the great adventure! What a tragedy that those of us of the "here and now" are alive in a time too premature to partake of the great spectacle to come. But perhaps the greater tragedy might be if our distant descendants cease to be, if the species ends, if no human being is alive to participate in the actualizing of the potentialities of mind and spirit.

Speculation like this aside, there is also the pragmatic consideration. Our history has already been written and not one tear will efface it. Our future is history that can be written with a guided pen. It would be the most unthinkable recklessness that, knowing the pen can be guided, it is not. But who will control the guiding? What part of the spectrum of Pleasura will guide the hand? That will be the result of point of view and its relative values, including valuation and recognition of absolute values.